PENGUIN BOOKS — GREAT IDEAS

An Attack on an Enemy of Freedom

Cicero
106–43 BC

Cicero

An Attack on an Enemy of Freedom

TRANSLATED BY
MICHAEL GRANT

PENGUIN BOOKS — GREAT IDEAS

PENGUIN BOOKS

Published by the Penguin Group
Penguin Books Ltd, 80 Strand, London WC2R 0RL, England
Penguin Group (USA) Inc., 375 Hudson Street, New York, New York 10014, USA
Penguin Group (Canada), 10 Alcorn Avenue, Toronto, Ontario, Canada M4V 3B2
(a division of Pearson Penguin Canada Inc.)
Penguin Ireland, 25 St Stephen's Green, Dublin 2, Ireland
(a division of Penguin Books Ltd)
Penguin Group (Australia), 250 Camberwell Road,
Camberwell, Victoria 3124, Australia (a division of Pearson Australia Group Pty Ltd)
Penguin Books India Pvt Ltd, 11 Community Centre,
Panchsheel Park, New Delhi – 110 017, India
Penguin Group (NZ), cnr Airborne and Rosedale Roads, Albany,
Auckland 1310, New Zealand (a division of Pearson New Zealand Ltd)
Penguin Books (South Africa) (Pty) Ltd, 24 Sturdee Avenue,
Rosebank 2196, South Africa

Penguin Books Ltd, Registered Offices: 80 Strand, London WC2R 0RL, England

www.penguin.com

Selected Works first published in Penguin Classics 1960
Selected Political Speeches first published in Penguin Classics 1969
These extracts published in Penguin Books 2005

1

Translation copyright © Michael Grant/Michael Grant Publications Ltd, 1960, 1969

Taken from the Penguin Classics editions *Selected Works* and *Selected Political Speeches*,
translated and edited by Michael Grant

Set by Rowland Phototypesetting Ltd, Bury St Edmunds, Suffolk
Printed in England by Clays Ltd, St Ives plc

Contents

The First Philippic against Mark Antony

Senators, before I offer the views on the political situation which the circumstances seem to me to demand, I will briefly indicate to you the reasons, first why I left Rome, and then why I turned back again.

As long as it still seemed possible to hope that you had resumed your control and authority over the government, I felt determined, as consul and Senator, to remain at my post. And so, from the day when we were summoned to meet in the Temple of Tellus, I made no journeys and never lifted my eyes from public affairs. In that temple I did all that was within my power to lay the foundations of peace. I reminded members of the ancient precedent created by the Athenians – making use in my oration of the Greek term which that state then employed to calm down civil strife – and I moved that every memory of our internal discords should be effaced in everlasting oblivion.

Mark Antony made a fine speech on that day, and his intentions were excellent. It was, indeed, he and his children who made it possible for peace to be established with the greatest of our fellow-citizens. What followed was in harmony with these beginnings. He held consultations on the national situation at his home, and invited the political leaders to attend. He offered admirable recommendations to the Senate. At that stage nothing was disinterred from Gaius Caesar's notebooks except matters that were generally known already. In his reply to every question Antony was completely direct. Were any exiles recalled? One, he said, and nobody else. Were any tax-exemptions granted? None, he replied. He even wanted us to accept the proposal of the illustrious Servius Sulpicius that no announcement should be posted of any decree or favour attributed to Caesar which had originated subsequently to the Ides of March. Of the many other excellent measures of Mark Antony I will say nothing, because I want to pass immediately to one particular admirable step that he took. The dictatorship, which had come to usurp virtually monarchical powers, was completely eliminated from the Roman constitution by his agency; we did not even debate the question. He brought us a draft of the decree he wanted the Senate to adopt, and when this was read out we accepted his proposal with the utmost enthusiasm, and passed a highly complimentary vote of thanks in his honour. The prospect ahead of us now seemed brilliant. For we had won liberation from the tyranny under which we had been labouring and, what is more, from all fears of similar tyranny in the future. Although there had often been legitimate dictators in the past, men could not forget the perpetual dictatorship of recent times, and by abolishing the entire office Mark Antony gave the state a mighty proof that he wanted our country to be free.

And then again, only a few days later, the Senate was delivered from the peril of a massacre when the runaway slave who had appropriated the name of Marius was executed and dragged away on a hook. All these deeds were performed jointly with his colleague; other things, later, were done by Dolabella alone, but I am sure that if his colleague had not been away these also would have been matters for collaboration. For during this period a most pernicious trouble was insinuating itself into the city and gaining strength day by day. The same men who had organized that travesty of a burial were now building a funeral monument in the Forum. Every day an increasing number of ruffians, together with their equally degraded slaves, menaced the dwellings and temples of the city with destruction. But these impudent criminal slaves, and their loathsome and infamous counterparts who were free, met their deserts from Dolabella when he pulled that accursed column down. So determined was his action that I am amazed by the contrast between that day and all the others which have followed.

For by the first of June, the date fixed for our meeting, you can see how everything had been transformed. Nothing was any longer done through the Senate, many significant measures were passed through the Assembly of the people – and others, what is more, without even consulting the Assembly, and against its wishes. The consuls elect declared they did not dare come into the Senate at all. The liberators of our country, too, were excluded from the very city which they had rescued from servitude – though the consuls simultaneously kept on praising them at public meetings and in private talk. Moreover, ex-soldiers claiming veteran rights, on whose behalf this Senate had shown great solicitude, were being egged on to cherish hopes of new plunder in addition to what they already possessed.

I came to the conclusion it was less disagreeable to hear of these things than to see them for myself; and, besides, I was entitled to go travelling on a special mission. This being so, I left Rome with the intention of being back by the first of the following January – which seemed the earliest likely date for a meeting of this body.

And so those, Senators, were the circumstances which prompted my departure. I will now indicate briefly the motives behind my return – which no doubt gives greater cause for surprise. After avoiding Brundisium and the usual route to Greece – as it was only sensible to do – I arrived on the first of August at Syracuse, since the crossing from there to Greece was well spoken of. But although I was associated with that city by the closest ties, I could not allow it to detain me for more than a single night, despite its desire to do so, because I was afraid that my sudden arrival among my friends there might arouse suspicion if I lingered. And so I proceeded with a fair wind to Leucopetra, which is a promontory in the district of Rhegium, and there I embarked to cross over to Greece.

But I had not gone very far when a southerly gale blew me back to my embarkation point. It was the middle of the night, and I stopped at the house of my friend and associate Publius Valerius. On the next day, while I was waiting there in the hope of a favourable wind, a number of citizens of Rhegium came to see me, including newcomers from Rome. They supplied my first news of Mark Antony's speech, which pleased me so much that after reading it I first began to consider the idea of returning to Rome. A little later the manifesto of Brutus and Cassius arrived, and it seemed to me – perhaps because I esteem them as national figures even more highly than as personal friends – a model of fair-mindedness. But bearers of good news have the habit of inventing additional points to give their message an even better welcome than it would otherwise receive, and so my informants added that an agreement was about to be reached, that there would be a well-attended meeting of the Senate on the first of August, and that Antony was going to drop his bad advisers, renounce his governorship of the Gallic provinces, and resume his allegiance to the authority of the Senate.

On hearing this I felt so enthusiastic to come back that no oars and no winds were speedy enough to satisfy my impatience – not that I imagined I would fail to return in time, but I was eager not to waste a moment in offering the government my congratulations. I made a quick passage to Velia, where I saw Brutus; though I found this a sorrowful meeting. I for my part was overcome by shame at the idea of returning to the city which Brutus had just left, and consenting to live there in security when he could not do the same. However, I did not find him as upset as I was myself. For he was exalted by the consciousness of his superb and magnificent deed. And he had no complaints to make about his own fate – but many about yours.

It was he who gave me my first information about Lucius Piso's speech in the Senate on August the first.

Piso had received little support, Brutus said, from the people who ought to have backed him. And yet in Brutus' opinion – which is the most authoritative view you could have – and according also to the complimentary comments of everyone I have spoken to since then, his effort was evidently a noble one. And so I hastened back to lend him my aid. My purpose was not so much to accomplish anything concrete, for such a thing I neither expected nor, in fact, achieved. But this is a time when many things contrary to the order of nature and even against the ordinary course of fate seem likely to happen at any moment, and, in case the doom that is common to all of us should come my way, I wanted to bequeath our country the sentiments I am now expressing, as a testimonial of my eternal devotion to its welfare.

Well, those, Senators, were the motives for my two successive courses of action, and I trust I have explained them to your satisfaction. And now, before I begin to speak about the political question, I feel obliged to enter a brief protest about the injustice Antony did me yesterday. I am his friend, and, because of a service he rendered me, I have always insisted on maintaining that this is so. Then why, I should like to know, did he show such unpleasantness in endeavouring to drag me to yesterday's Senate meeting? Was I the only absentee? Were the numbers of those present lower than on many previous occasions? Did the matter under discussion attain the degree of gravity which has sometimes in the past meant that even sick men had to be carried to meetings? Are you telling me that Hannibal himself was at the gates?

Or perhaps we were considering the question of peace with Pyrrhus – since that, tradition records, was the debate for which the great Appius, blind and old, had himself carried into the Senate. But no: the motion was about public thanksgivings, and that is a subject for which Senators are not usually in short supply. Securities need not be called for to guarantee their attendance, since this is ensured by their eagerness to show goodwill to the proposed recipients of the honour; and the same applies when a Triumph is being discussed. On such occasions the consuls can afford to be so indifferent that a Senator is virtually free to attend or not as he pleases.

I knew that this was the practice; and I was tired after my journey, and not very well. So for friendship's sake I sent a message to inform Antony. Whereupon he declared, in your hearing, that he would come to my house with a demolition squad. This was a remarkably ill-tempered and immoderate way to talk. Whatever sort of an offence did he suppose he was penalizing by this harsh declaration, in the presence of the Senators, of his intention to use state employees to demolish a residence that had been erected at state expense in accordance with a decision of the Senate? Never has compulsion been applied to a Senator by any sanction as severe as that. Indeed, the only known penalties are a security or a fine. Besides, had he known the opinion I should have expressed if I had in fact attended, I am sure he would have wanted to relax the rigour of his coercive attitude quite a bit!

For you cannot imagine, gentlemen, that the decree you yesterday passed so unwillingly would have had my

support. For that decree involved the confusion of a
thanksgiving with a sacrifice in honour of the dead, and
the insertion of sacrilegious procedures into the state
religion – for such was the effect of proclaiming a thanksgiving in honour of a man who was no longer alive. The
question of his identity is neither here nor there. Even if
he were that famous Brutus himself, the man who by
his own hand liberated the country from the tyranny of
royal rule, whose descendants have maintained the same
tradition of active heroism for very nearly five hundred
years, still nothing would induce me to equate a dead
human being with the immortal gods by awarding him
a public thanksgiving when he should instead have had
honours rendered to him in his grave. No, the vote
I should have cast would have been one capable of
justification to the Roman people in case some outstanding catastrophe such as a war or a plague or a famine
overtook the country. For some of these disasters have
already actually come about; while the rest, I fear, are
impending. But as it is, all I can do about yesterday's
decree is entreat the gods to pardon the people of Rome,
who in any case do not like the measure – and to pardon
the Senate that only passed it with reluctance.

Well, as regards our other political ills, am I permitted
to offer my observations? For I regard myself at liberty
(and always shall) to fight in defence of my own position,
and to think nothing of death; and that will always be
my attitude. Only give me free access to this place, and
I am prepared to express my thoughts whatever the risk.

Well, gentlemen, I wish after all it had been possible
for me to attend on August the first! Not that it would

have been any use, but then at least there would not have been, as there was, only one isolated consul whose behaviour lived up to his own high rank and his country's needs. How sad that the men who had received Rome's greatest favours failed to support Lucius Piso in his truly admirable motion! Was it for this meagre result that the people of Rome made us consuls? Were we supposed to enjoy the highest position that the state is able to confer, and yet remain entirely oblivious of the national inter-ests? For not one single former consul supported Lucius Piso either by word of mouth or even by the expression on his face!

Curse it, do you have to be voluntary slaves? I grant you that a measure of servility may formerly have been unavoidable. And I am also prepared to concede that my criticism need not apply to every consular speaker indiscriminately. For I distinguish between certain people whose silence I excuse and others who I feel are under an obligation to speak out. The latter category, I regret to say, has incurred suspicion in the eyes of the Roman people. This is not so much because they are frightened, though such a thing would certainly be shameful, but because for whatever reasons – and these are various – they have fallen short of what their eminent status demands.

First of all, therefore, I want to express the warm grati-tude I feel towards Piso, who was undeterred by the practical limitations of what he could achieve for his country, and thought only of what his duty demanded that he should attempt. And then, as to my next point,

Senators, I realize you may not feel sufficiently intrepid to support the point of view and course of action which I am now going to urge upon you. Nevertheless, I ask you to continue to listen with the same goodwill that you have shown me up to this point.

To begin with, then, I hold that the acts of Caesar ought to be retained. I say this not because I approve of them: for who could do that? No, I say it because I attach supreme importance to peace and tranquillity. I wish Mark Antony were here today (though I should prefer his advisers to remain elsewhere!). But I suppose he has the right to be unwell – even if yesterday he did not allow it to myself. If he were here, he would tell me, or rather he would tell you, Senators, what line he adopts as regards the justification of Caesar's acts. The point is this: are the acts we are being asked to ratify the ones that are jotted down in scrappy memoranda and handwritten scrawls and notebooks produced on the sole authority of Antony – or rather not even produced but merely quoted – whereas the acts that Caesar himself engraved on brass tablets, with the intention of preserving the national Assembly's directions and definitive laws, are to be totally disregarded? My own view is that nothing forms such an indissoluble part of Caesar's acts as the laws which were adopted on Caesar's proposal. But if, on the other hand, he once made some promise or other to somebody, does that also really have to be regarded as irrevocable, even though he was never able to give effect to it himself? It is true that in his lifetime he offered many promises which he did not, in fact, fulfil. But these promises of his which have been dug up after his death are so immensely numerous that they exceed the entire total of the favours he actually dispensed for services rendered, or as free gifts, during all the years of his life.

All the same, it is not by any means my intention to tamper with any of those items; I do not even propose to touch them. On the contrary, I am an enthusiastic defender of his excellent acts. For example, I sincerely wish that the funds he collected in the Temple of Ops were still there this day. Blood-stained that money certainly was, but since it cannot be restored to its owners we could make good use of it today. However, let us put up with its dissipation – if it is a fact that this is what his acts laid down.

But surely the most important of all the acts of a civil officer of state, conducting the government through the powers vested in his person, are the laws which were passed on his initiative. Look for the acts of Gaius Gracchus; you will find the Sempronian laws. Consider the acts of Sulla; the Cornelian laws are what you see. Or think of the third consulship of Pompeius – what acts did that produce? Surely his legislation again. If you asked Caesar himself to describe his acts at Rome and in civil life, he would answer that he had sponsored many first-rate laws. But his handwritten notes, on the other hand, he would either regard as provisional and liable to emendation, or he would omit to produce them at all, or even if he produced them he would not wish for their inclusion among his acts. However, that is a point on which I am prepared, in certain instances, to give way and turn a blind eye. But the most important aspect of the matter relates to his laws, and in so far as they are concerned I am by no means ready to tolerate the annulment of Caesar's acts.

Take, for example, that exceptionally salutary and valuable law, frequently longed for in the happy days of the Republic, which provides that former praetors should not govern provinces for longer than a year, and former consuls for not more than two. Suppress this law, and how can you still speak of preserving Caesar's acts? And then again this bill that has been published about a third panel of judges – surely it rescinds Caesar's entire legislation relating to those panels. If you are going to abolish Caesar's laws how on earth can you say you defend his acts? For it is totally illogical to suggest that everything he jotted down in a notebook to help his memory, however unjust and useless, must be regarded as part of his acts, whereas what he actually had passed by the people, voting in its Assembly of Centuries, is not going to be included among them at all.

But let us see what this new third panel is. It consists of centurions, Antony says. Well, they were authorized to serve as judges, were they not, by a Julian law, and before that by Pompeian and Aurelian laws. So they did serve: and not only in cases concerning a centurion but a Roman knight as well – and so it has come about that gentlemen of great valour and repute, former commanders of troops, have served as judges in the past and still do so to this day. 'But those are not the men I am concerned with,' he continues. 'I want everyone who has ever commanded a unit of a hundred men to be a judge.' Even if you applied this principle to everyone who had served as a knight, which is after all a more distinguished rank, the argument would still be totally unconvincing. For when you appoint a judge it is perfectly proper to be guided by considerations of property and rank. 'But such qualifications do not interest me,' answers Antony. 'Indeed, I am proposing that judges should be taken from another category also: from private soldiers of the Legion of the Lark. For without such a measure our supporters are sure they will suffer victimization.' But what an insult to these people whom (though nothing was further from their thoughts) you are proposing to mobilize as judges! For what your law implies is that the third panel is going to consist of members who will not dare to produce impartial verdicts. But, heavens, what a miscalculation on the part of the people who thought up the law! For what in fact will happen is that people of no standing who are now to be included among the judges will try to force themselves up out of their obscurity by producing the strictest possible decisions – calculating that these can get them promoted to grander panels instead of the undistinguished one to which, quite rightly, they had been allotted.

Another bill that has now been published rules that men convicted of violence and treason shall have the right to appeal to the Assembly. But, I ask you, is this a law at all – is it not rather a law to end all laws? And anyway, who cares nowadays whether this bill is persevered with or not? For there is not, in fact, one single person today awaiting trial under the laws concerned with those offences. And I do not suppose that there will be anyone in the future either – since acts perpetrated by people under arms will clearly never be brought into court!

But the measure, we are told, is a popular one. What a good thing it would be if you really had something popular in mind! For in our present circumstances, Roman citizens are unanimous in their estimate of the country's political needs. So I cannot understand your enthusiasm to propose a law which, far from being a source of popularity, is bound to earn you discredit. For it is in the highest degree discreditable that a man who has committed violence and treason against the Roman people, and suffered condemnation for those offences, should forthwith be allowed to relapse into precisely the same violent behaviour which was responsible for his conviction. However, it is a waste of time to go on arguing about the proposed law. For obviously its real concern is not with the question of appeal at all. Its object, and your object in bringing it forward, is to prevent any and every prosecution under the laws in question. For how could one ever find a prosecutor idiotic enough to secure a conviction and thus expose himself to hostile crowds on someone else's payroll, or a judge rash enough to pronounce a sentence which will get him dragged before a gang of bribed toughs?

No, the bill is not really designed to give a right of appeal. What it does instead is to hand over two particularly useful laws and courts to suppression. In other words it offers young men a clear invitation to become riotous, seditious, pernicious citizens. One hesitates to think of the ruinous excesses to which rabid tribunes will be encouraged to go when these two courts for violence and treason are no more. Besides, the measure will also have the effect of superseding the laws of Caesar which rule that men convicted of the two offences in question become outlaws banned from water and fire. Because, surely, to allow people condemned for these crimes to appeal is tantamount to declaring that these acts of Caesar are abolished. Although I personally was never in favour of his acts, gentlemen, I nevertheless maintained that for unity's sake they ought to be kept intact. That is why I maintain that nothing should be done at this juncture to annul the laws he sponsored in his lifetime – or even, for that matter, the ones you now see published and posted after his death.

It is true that exiles are recalled from banishment – by a man who is dead. A dead man, again, has conferred citizenship, not merely on individuals but on entire nations and provinces. A dead man has wiped out national revenues, by unlimited grants of exemption. And yet, even so, I assert my willingness to defend these measures, even when they are only guaranteed by a single individual's authority (a substantial authority, admittedly) and produced from his own house. But, if this is accepted, how on earth can we simultaneously urge the suppression of laws which Caesar himself read out in our presence and published and proposed, laws about provinces and about courts which he was well content to sponsor and considered indispensable to our national interests? When laws are publicly announced, as those were, at least we are afforded a chance to complain if we want to. But when we merely have to rely on hearsay to discover that a law has been passed at all, no such opportunity exists. And the laws produced by Antony were passed without any prior advertisement whatever: we were not even shown a preliminary draft.

There is no reason, it is true, Senators, why I myself, or any of you, need have the slightest fear of bad laws being adopted so long as good tribunes are available. And we do possess such tribunes, men ready to apply their veto, ready to use their sacred office in defence of the constitution. Obviously we ought, then, to lack the slightest grounds for apprehension. 'But what is this veto,' asks Antony, 'what sacred office are you talking about?' The answer is that the right of veto, and the office to which I refer, are institutions fundamental to the security of the state. 'That does not impress us at all,' Antony comments. 'We regard it as old-fashioned and stupid. What we shall do is to barricade the Forum and close all its entrances; detachments of armed men will be posted at numerous points.'

And then, I suppose, what is transacted in that fashion will be law. And you will give orders to have bronze tablets engraved with the legal formula 'the consuls by right of law put the question to the people'. But how can you call this the same right of putting the question which our forefathers handed down to us? The formula continues, 'and the people by right of law passed the measure'. Which people? The ones who were shut out? And what right of law? The law which armed violence has obliterated out of existence?

These observations are intended as guidance for the future – since it is the duty of a friend to offer advance warning against things that can still be avoided. If these unfortunate occurrences never materialize, then my comments will automatically be refuted. The bills I am talking about are ones which are going to be published in due form, and there is nothing to stop you from proposing whatever you like. But as for myself, I consider it my duty to forecast possible flaws and ask you for their removal – to denounce, in other words, armed violence, and to demand its elimination!

When patriotic motives impel me, Dolabella, to offer such suggestions, I am justified in hoping that you consuls will not take it amiss. I do not imagine that you yourself will be angry, since I know what a good-tempered man you are. But people are commenting that your colleague Mark Antony, as he luxuriates in his present position which he regards as so fine (though I would hold him more fortunate, to put it mildly, if he modelled his consulship on those of his grandfathers and his maternal uncle), has taken offence. Now it is far from agreeable, I can see, when a man who has something against you holds a weapon in his hand – especially now that swords can be used with such impunity. But I will propose a pact: it seems to me a fair arrangement and I do not believe Antony will turn it down. That is to say, if I utter one single insulting remark about his private life or his morals I shall not object to him treating me as a bitter enemy. But if, on the other hand, I merely adhere to the custom of my entire political career and pronounce my frank opinion about national issues, first of all I beg him not to be indignant with me, and next, if that plea fails, I at least urge that his indignation should only be that of one fellow-citizen against another. Let him by all means employ an armed guard if this is needed, as he claims, for self-defence; but do not let their weapons be used on people who are expressing their views on public affairs. Now, what could be a fairer request than that? However, if any and every speech which goes against his wishes causes him to take umbrage even though it may contain not a trace of an insult – and some of his friends have told me that this is what happens – then we shall just have to put up with our friend's disposition and leave it at that. But these same henchmen of Antony also advise me, 'You as an opponent of Caesar will not be allowed the same indulgence as Piso, who was the father of his wife.' And at the same time they give me a word of warning which I do not propose to neglect, and it is this: being ill has not served me as an excuse for absence from the Senate – but I shall have a better excuse if I am dead!

You are my intimate friend, Dolabella; and, when I see you sitting there, heaven knows I find it impossible to keep silent about the mistake that you are both making. Each of you is a nobleman with lofty aims, and I must part company with those who maintain, in their excessive credulity, that it is money you are after; for that is something which men of true greatness and renown have always despised. I refuse to believe that what you want is wealth acquired by violent means, or the sort of power that Romans would find intolerable. Yours, I am convinced, is the very different ambition of gaining the love of your fellow-citizens and winning a splendid reputation. Such a reputation means praise won by noble actions and by great services to one's country, and endorsed by the testimony of national leaders and the whole population. And I would be prepared to enlarge further, Dolabella, on this subject of the rewards won by splendid deeds, did I not see that in these recent times you yourself have shown that you appreciate this very matter even better than anyone else.

For you can surely remember no happier occasion in all your life than the day on which, before returning home, you cleaned up the Forum, dispersed that concourse of blasphemous scoundrels, punished the ringleaders for their loathsome designs, and rescued the city from incendiarism and the menace of massacre. All members of the community, whatever their rank or class or station, pressed forward to compliment and congratulate you. Indeed, loyal citizens were even thanking and congratulating me as your proxy; because they believed your deed had been instigated by myself. Cast your mind back, I urge you, Dolabella, to that unanimous demonstration in the theatre when the entire crowd of spectators, dismissing from their minds what they had held against you previously, revealed that your recent action on their behalf had made them put aside all recollection of their earlier grudges.

And so it distresses me deeply, Dolabella, that after winning such great respect you should now be prepared to cast this all aside with complete equanimity.

And as for you, Mark Antony, you are not with us now, but I have an appeal to address to you all the same. That one day, on which the Senate met in the temple of Tellus, must surely have happier memories for you than all the subsequent months in which so many people (greatly differing from me) have accounted you fortunate. For what a splendid speech you made about national unity! When you renounced your hostility towards your fellow-consul and forgot the unfavourable auspices which you yourself as an augur of Rome had declared to be an impediment to his election: when you accepted him for the first time as your colleague, and sent your infant son to the Capitol as a hostage, your words freed the ex-soldiers from all apprehensions about their position, and indeed delivered our entire nation from its anxieties. Never has there been more rejoicing than there was on that day, both in the Senate and among the whole people of Rome – which was gathered together in numbers such as had never been seen at any public meeting before. At that juncture it finally and definitely seemed true that the action of those most valiant citizens had brought us our liberty, because their wish had come true, and the outcome of liberation was peace.

And then again on the next day and the second and the third and those that followed, you daily continued to confer some fresh gift upon your country; and the greatest of all these benefits was your abolition of the title of dictator. For that was the time when you (of all people) branded the dead Caesar's memory with ineradicable infamy. In a bygone age the crime of a single Marcus Manlius caused the Manlian family to decree that no patrician Manlius should ever again bear the first name of Marcus. And now, by the same token, the detestation felt for a single dictator caused you to suppress the name of dictator altogether.

But then, after these outstanding services that you had contributed to the nation, whatever can have happened? Did you regret the good fortune and illustriousness and glory and renown you had won? I wonder how that sudden transformation came about. I cannot bring myself to suspect you were corrupted by financial considerations. Let people say what they like, one is not forced to believe them: and I have never found anything squalid or mean in your character. It is true that the people in a man's home sometimes deprave him – but I know very well that you are a strong-minded person. I am only sorry that your freedom from guilt is not equalled by your freedom from suspicion.

But what frightens me more than such imputations is the possibility that you yourself may disregard the true path of glory, and instead consider it glorious to possess more power than all your fellow-citizens combined – preferring that they should fear you rather than like you. If that is what you think, your idea of where the road of glory lies is mistaken. For glory consists of being regarded with affection by one's country, winning praise and respect and love; whereas to be feared and disliked, on the other hand, is unpleasant and hateful and debilitating and precarious. This is clear enough from the play in which the man said, 'Let them hate provided that they fear'. He found to his cost that such a policy was his ruin. It would have been so much better, Mark Antony, if you had kept the record of your grandfather before your eyes. You have heard me speak of him at length and on numerous occasions. Do you think *he* would have regarded his claim to immortality as being best served by terrorizing people with armed gangs? No, what life and good fortune meant to him was to be the equal of everybody else in freedom, but their superior in his honourable way of life. About his glorious successes I shall say nothing now; but I want to record my conviction that the last tragic day of his life was preferable to the tyranny of Lucius Cinna who brutally slew him.

However, I see no hope of influencing you by what I say. For if the end that befell Gaius Caesar does not persuade you that it is better to inspire affection than terror, no words that anyone could utter will have the slightest effect or success. People who say Caesar was enviable are profoundly misguided. For no one can be said to have a happy life when its violent termination brings his slayers not merely impunity but the height of glory. So change your ways, I entreat you. Remember your ancestors – and govern our country in such a way that your fellow-citizens will rejoice that you were born. For without that there is no such thing as happiness, or renown, or security.

Your fellow-Romans have furnished you both with ample warnings, and it worries me that they fail to impress you sufficiently. Think of the clamour raised by countless citizens at gladiatorial shows, think of all the versified popular slogans, think of those endless acclamations in front of the statue of Pompeius, think of the two tribunes who are against you! Surely these are sufficient indications that every Roman speaks with a single voice! And then again did you attach no importance to the applause at Apollo's Games? – or rather I should call it the testimony and judgement of the entire Roman people. What an honour for the men who were prevented by armed violence from being present in person – though they were present in the hearts and emotions of the people of Rome! Or did you really suppose that all that approval was meant for the playwright Accius – that his tragedy was winning a belated prize sixty years after its first performance? No, Brutus was the man for whom the cheering and the prize were intended. He could not himself attend the games that were displayed in his name, but the Romans who witnessed that sumptuous show paid their tribute to him in his absence, and sought to comfort the sadness which they felt because their liberator was not with them by incessant cheers and shouts of sympathy.

Personally I have always despised applause of this kind – when its recipients are the sort of men who will do anything to win popularity. All the same, when the cheering comes unanimously from the highest and middle and lowest classes of the community alike, and when the politicians who used to bow to the popular will are suddenly found going in the opposite direction, that seems to me to constitute not merely applause but a verdict!

Or if you regard that as a trivial matter – although it is actually most significant – do you also attach no importance to the proof you have seen of Rome's loving solicitude for the health of Aulus Hirtius? It was already a very notable fact that Roman people esteem him as they do, that unique affection is lavished on him by his friends, that his family hold him so exceptionally dear. But now, in his illness, is there anyone in the memory of mankind who has been the object of such profound anxiety among all good citizens, and of such universal alarm? Nobody has ever been favoured with such demonstrations before. And so does it not occur to you that the people who are so deeply concerned for the lives of those they hope will serve the state may start having thoughts about your own lives as well?

Senators, the rewards I hoped to gain from my return are now mine. For the views I have expressed to you today are a guarantee that, whatever may happen in the future, my determination shall be on record. Moreover, you have given me an attentive and sympathetic hearing. If, without peril to myself and you, I am allowed further opportunities to speak, I shall use them as often as I can. If not, I shall work to the best of my ability for the welfare not of my own self but of our country. Meanwhile, I can say that my life has now lasted long enough, by the measure of years and fame alike. If an additional span is now to be vouchsafed to me, I shall again not devote it to my own interests, but it will be placed, as before, at the disposal of yourselves and Rome.

Attack on an Enemy of Freedom
(The Second Philippic Against Mark Antony)

Members of the Senate: Why is this my fate? I am obliged to record that, for twenty years past, our country has never had an enemy who has not, simultaneously, made himself an enemy of mine as well. I need mention no names. You remember the men for yourselves. They have paid me graver penalties than I could have wished.

Antony, you are modelling your actions on theirs. So what happened to them ought to frighten you; I am amazed that it does not. When those others were against me as well as against Rome I was less surprised. For they did not seek me out as an enemy. No, it was I who, for patriotic reasons, took the initiative against every one of them. But you I have never injured, even in words. And yet, without provocation, you have assailed me with gross insults. Catiline himself could not have been so outrageous, nor Publius Clodius so hysterical. Evidently you felt that the way to make friends, in disreputable circles, was by breaking off relations with me.

Did you take this step in a spirit of contempt? I should not have thought that my life, and my reputation, and my qualities – such as they are – provide suitable material for Antony's contempt. Nor can he have believed, surely, that he could successfully disparage me before the Senate. Accustomed though it is to complimenting distinguished Romans for good service to the state, the Senate has praised only one man for actually rescuing it from annihilation: and that is myself. But perhaps Antony's ambition was to compete with me as a speaker? If so, how extremely generous of him to present me with such a subject – justification of myself, criticism of him: the richest and most promising theme imaginable! No, the truth is clearly this. He saw no chance of proving to people like himself that he was Rome's enemy, unless he became mine too.

Before I reply to his other accusations, I should like to say a few words in answer to one particular complaint, namely that it was I who broke our friendship. Because I regard this as a very serious charge. He has protested that I once spoke against him in a lawsuit. But surely I was obliged to support my close friend against someone with whom I had no connexion. Besides, the backer of my friend's opponent was only interested in him from a discreditable interest in his youthfulness, and not because the young man was really promising. Since his supporter had procured an unfair result through a scandalous exercise of the veto, I had no choice but to intervene. However, I think I know why you brought the matter up. You wanted to ingratiate yourself with the underworld, by reminding everybody that you are the son-in-law of an ex-slave, Quintus Fadius; in other words, a former slave is the grandfather of your children.

Yet you allege that you constantly visited my house, in order to receive my tuition. If you had, your reputation and your morals would have benefited. But you did not! Even if you had wanted to, Gaius Scribonius Curio would never have let you. Then you claim that you retired from the election to the augurship in my favour. That is sheer effrontery: monstrous, shameless, and unbelievable. In those days, when the entire Board of Augurs was pressing me to become a member, and my nominators (only two being allowed) were Pompey and Quintus Hortensius, you were completely destitute. There was only one hope of safety which you could see, and that was revolution. At that juncture you stood no chance whatever of becoming an augur; for Curio was out of Italy. Later, when you came up for election, you could not have secured the votes of a single tribe without Curio. So energetic, indeed, was the canvassing of his friends on your behalf, that they were condemned in the courts for the use of violence!

You did me a favour, you object. Certainly; I have always admitted the instance that you quote. It seemed to me less undesirable to admit my obligation to you than to let ignorant people think me ungrateful. However, the favour was this, was it not? – that you did not kill me at Brundisium. But I do not see how you could have killed me. For I had been ordered to Italy by the conqueror himself – the very man whose chief gangster you were congratulating yourself on having become.

Nevertheless, let us imagine that you could have killed me. That, Senators, is what a favour from gangsters amounts to. They refrain from murdering someone; then they boast that they have spared him! If that is a true favour, then those who killed Caesar, after he had spared them, would never have been regarded as so glorious – and they are men whom you yourself habitually describe as noble. But the mere abstention from a dreadful crime is surely no sort of favour. In the situation in which this 'favour' placed me, my dominant feelings ought not to have been pleasure because you did not kill me, but sorrow because you could have done so with impunity.

However, let us even assume that it was a favour; at any rate the best favour that a gangster could confer. Still, in what respect can you call me ungrateful? Were my protests against the downfall of our country wrong, because you might think they showed ingratitude? I admit that there was no lack of grief and misery in my complaints. But a man in my position, the position conferred on me by the Senate and people of Rome, could not help that. And my words were restrained and friendly, never insulting. Surely that is real moderation – to protest about Antony and yet refrain from abuse!

For what was left of Rome, Antony, owed its final annihilation to yourself. In your home everything had a price: and a truly sordid series of deals it was. Laws you passed, laws you caused to be put through in your interests, had never even been formally proposed. You admitted this yourself. You were an augur, yet you never took the auspices. You were a consul, yet you blocked the legal right of other officials to exercise the veto. Your armed escort was shocking. You are a drink-sodden, sex-ridden wreck. Never a day passes in that ill-reputed house of yours without orgies of the most repulsive kind.

In spite of all that, I restricted myself in my speech to solemn complaints concerning the state of our nation. I said nothing personal about the man. I might have been conducting a case against Marcus Licinius Crassus (as I often have, on grave issues) instead of against this utterly loathsome gladiator.

Today, therefore, I am going to ensure that he understands what a favour I, on that occasion, conferred upon himself. He read out a letter, this creature, which he said I had sent him. But he has absolutely no idea how to behave – how other people behave. Who, with the slightest knowledge of decent people's habits, could conceivably produce letters sent him by a friend, and read them in public, merely because some quarrel has arisen between him and the other? Such conduct strikes at the roots of human relations; it means that absent friends are excluded from communicating with each other. For men fill their letters with flippancies which appear tasteless if they are published – and with serious matters which are quite unsuitable for wide circulation. Antony's action proves he is totally uncivilized.

But just see how unbelievably stupid he is as well. Try to answer my next point, you marvel of eloquence! (At least that is what you seem to Seius Mustela and Numisius Tiro, who stand here in full view of the Senate at this very moment, sword in hand: and even I shall admit that you are an eloquent orator after you explain to me how, when they were charged with assassination, you could get them acquitted.) However, to resume – what if I denied that I had ever sent you that letter? You would be left without an answer: you could not find a shred of evidence to convict me. By the handwriting? It is true that you have found your knowledge of handwriting very lucrative. All the same, your efforts would be pointless, because the letter was written by a secretary. What a lucky man your teacher of oratory was! You paid him very handsomely (as I shall remind you later), and yet when you left his hands you were still a complete fool. To charge one's opponent with something which, in the face of a blank denial, he cannot press home to the slightest effect is of no service whatever to any speaker; indeed to anyone with any sense at all. Nevertheless I do not deny authorship. And when I say that, I am also saying that you are not ill-behaved but a lunatic. For my whole letter was replete with dutiful kindness – it was a veritable model of how to behave. Your criticism concerning its contents merely amounts to this: that I do not express a bad opinion of you; and that I address you as a Roman citizen and a decent man, instead of as a bandit and a criminal.

Now I do not propose to produce *your* letter, though under this provocation I should be entitled to: the letter in which you begged me to consent to someone's return from exile, and promised that you would not bring him back unless I agreed. And I did agree. For it was not for me to stand in the way of your outrageous behaviour, seeing that this is uncontrollable even by the authority of this Senatorial Order, and universal public opinion, and the whole body of the law. But what was the point of making me such a plea, when Caesar had actually passed a law authorizing the return of the very man with whom your letter was concerned? No doubt Antony was eager that I should get the credit! – seeing that even he was not going to win any credit, since the matter had already been settled by legislation.

Senators: in self-defence, and in denunciation of Antony, I have no lack of material. But as regards the former of those themes, I have an appeal to make: while I speak in my own defence I urge you to be indulgent. The second matter I shall look after on my own account – I shall ensure that what I am going to say against Antony impresses itself upon your attention. At the same time I beg this of you. My whole career as a speaker, indeed my whole life, has, I believe, demonstrated to you that I am a moderate man and not an extremist. So do not suppose that I have forgotten myself when I reply to this man in the spirit in which he has challenged me. I am not going to treat him as a consul, for he did not treat me as a former consul, as a man of consular rank. Besides, he is no true consul at all. He does not live like one; he does not work like one; and he was never elected to be one. Whereas a former consul I unquestionably am.

You can see what sort of a consul he claims to be by the way in which he criticizes my tenure of that office. Yet my consulship, Senators, though it can be called mine, was in plain fact yours. For everything I decided, every policy I carried out, every action I took, derived from this Senatorial Order – from its deliberations, its authority, and its rulings. What a strange kind of wisdom you show, Antony – eloquence is evidently not your only quality – when you abuse me before the very men whose corporate judgement inspired those actions of mine! The only people who have ever abused my consulship are Publius Clodius and yourself. And his fate – the fate which also overtook Curio – will be yours: for what brought death to both of them is now in your home!*

So Antony disapproves of my consulship. But – to name first the most recently deceased of the ex-consuls of that time – Publius Servilius Vatia Isauricus thought well of it. Quintus Lutatius Catulus, who will always carry weight among our countrymen, likewise bestowed upon me his approval. So did Lucius Licinius Lucullus and his brother Marcus, and Marcus Licinius Crassus, Quintus Hortensius, Gaius Scribonius Curio the elder, Gaius Calpurnius Piso, Manius Acilius Glabrio, Manius Aemilius Lepidus, Lucius Volcacius Tullus, Gaius Marcius Figulus, and the two consuls designate at the time, Decimus Junius Silanus and Lucius Licinius Murena. And Marcus Porcius Cato felt the same as those of consular rank: he too praised my activities as consul. *Your* consulship, on the other hand, was the worst of the many things which death spared Cato. Another very strong supporter of mine was Pompey. When we first met after his return from Syria, he embraced me, offered his congratulations, and declared that it was through my services that there was still a Rome for him to see. But why do I mention individuals? A very full house of the Senate so warmly applauded my consulship that there was not a man there who did not thank me as if I had been his father. Their possessions, their lives, their children's lives, their country – they owed all these, said every one of them, to me.

However, since Rome has lost all the great men whom I have mentioned, let us pass to the two ex-consuls of

* Fulvia, successively the wife of Publius Clodius, Curio, and Antony.

that time who are still with us. For those very actions which you denounce, that brilliant statesman Lucius Aurelius Cotta proposed that I should be accorded a most generous vote of thanks. And this proposal was adopted – by those very ex-consuls whose names I have just recorded, and indeed by the whole Senate. This was an honour which, ever since the city's foundation, had been awarded to no civilian before me. On that occasion your uncle Lucius Julius Caesar attacked his sister's husband, your stepfather; and he spoke with great eloquence, solemnity, and firmness. In all your activities throughout your whole life, your inspiration, your teacher, ought to have been Lucius Caesar. But instead of your uncle, the man on whom you preferred to model yourself was your stepfather. When I was consul I consulted Lucius Caesar, though we were not related. You are his sister's son: but when did you ever consult him on state affairs?

Who, indeed, are Antony's advisers? Evidently people whose birthdays have not come to our attention. Antony is not attending the Senate today. Why? He is giving a birthday-party on his estate. For whom? I shall name no names. No doubt it is some comic Phormio or other, some Gnatho or Ballio.* What a disgusting, intolerable sensualist the man is, as well as a vicious, unsavoury crook! How is it possible, Antony, that you should consistently fail to consult that admirable leading Senator Lucius Caesar, who is your close relation, while instead

---

* Phormio and Gnatho were parasites in the *Phormio* and *Eunuch* respectively, comedies by Terence (*c.* 195–159 BC). Ballio was the pimp in *The Cheat* by Plautus (*c.* 254–184 BC).

you prefer to rely on the advice of this collection of down-and-out spongers?

I see; *your* consulship is beneficent, *mine* was destructive. Your impudence must be equal to your debauchery if you dare make that assertion in the very place where, as consul, I consulted the Senate, which once, in its glory, presided over the whole world: namely, in this temple of Concord, now crammed – by your agency – with delinquents bristling with weapons. And yet you had the effrontery, the unlimited effrontery, to claim that, when I was consul, the road up the Capitoline Hill was packed with armed slaves! Do you really mean to suggest that I was applying violent pressure upon the Senate in order to force through those decrees of mine – in other words, that they were discreditable? You poor fool, to utter such impertinences before men of this calibre! – if the facts are known to you: or perhaps they are not, since all that is good is completely foreign to your mind.

When the Senate met in this temple, every single Roman knight, every young man of aristocratic birth – except yourself – every man (of whatever class) who was conscious of his Roman citizenship, gathered together on the road to the Capitol; each of them gave in his name. So many were they that no number of secretaries or writing tablets could have been enough for the registration of the entire multitude of them.

For that was the very moment when evil men were confessing that they had planned to assassinate their country. The revelations of their own accomplices had forced them to this admission. So had their own handwriting, and the almost audible testimony of their own letters. To murder the citizens of Rome – that was the intention which emerged; to ravage Italy; revolution! At such a time, no one could fail to hear the call to defend the common cause – especially as the Senate and Roman people, in those days, possessed a leader. If they had his like as a leader now, the fate that descended upon those anarchists would be yours also.

Antony protests that I refused to give up his step-father's body for burial. But even Publius Clodius never brought that charge. I was the enemy of Clodius – justifiably: but your faults, I regret to see, are blacker even than his. Why did it occur to you, I wonder, to remind us of your upbringing in your stepfather's home? I suppose you were afraid that we should be sceptical of nature's unaided effects; that we should need this evidence of upbringing before we could understand why you had turned out so criminally.

Really, your speech was demented, it was so full of inconsistencies. From beginning to end, you were not merely incoherent but glaringly self-contradictory: indeed you contradicted yourself more often than you contradicted me. You admitted that your stepfather was involved in that terrible crime, and yet you complained because he had been punished for what he did. But the effect of that argument was to praise my part in the matter, and to blame what was wholly the Senate's part. For whereas it was I who arrested the guilty men, it was the Senate which punished them. So our masterly speaker here does not realize he is praising the man he is trying to attack, and is abusing those who sit here listening to him!

I will not call this effrontery – which is in any case a quality he proudly claims. But Antony has no desire to be stupid, and he must be the most stupid man alive to talk of the Capitoline road at this moment – when armed men are actually standing here among our benches, are stationed with their swords in that same temple of Concord, heaven bear me witness, where my consulship saw decisions which saved our nation and brought us in safety to this day.

Go on, criticize the Senate, criticize the knights who were at that time its partners. Assail every class and every citizen with your accusations, provided you admit that at the present moment this meeting of ours here is picketed by your Ituraean police. Unscrupulousness is not what prompts these shameless statements of yours; you make them because you entirely fail to grasp how you are contradicting yourself. In fact, you must be an imbecile. How could a sane person first take up arms to destroy his country, and then protest because someone else had armed himself to save it?

At one point you tried to be witty. Heaven knows this did not suit you. And your failure is particularly blameworthy, since you could have acquired some wit from that professional actress known as your wife. 'Let gown be mightier than sword'* were the words of mine that you mocked. Well, that was so in those days, was it not? But since then your swords have won. Let us consider which was the better: the time when gangsters'

* A quotation from Cicero's much maligned poem *On his Consulate*. The verse went on: 'let laurel yield to honest worth.'

36

weapons were overcome by men defending Roman freedom, or now, when your weapons have struck that
freedom down. As far as my poem is concerned that is
the only answer I have to give. I will merely add briefly
that you understand neither this poem nor any other
literature. I, on the other hand, though I have not neglected my duty to our country or to my friends, have
nevertheless employed my leisure hours in literary pro-
ductions of many kinds. All that I have written, the
whole of my effort, has been intended for the benefit of
young people and for the greater glory of Rome. However, that is another matter. Let us turn to questions of
more importance.

It was upon my initiative, you said, that Publius
Clodius was killed by Titus Annius Milo. But what would
people have thought if he had been killed when, sword
in hand, *you* chased him into the Forum, with the whole
of Rome looking on? If he had not stopped you by hiding
under the stairs of a bookshop and barricading them,
you would have finished him off. Now I admit that I
viewed your attempt with favour; yet even you do not
claim that I prompted you. But as for Milo, I did not
have an opportunity even to favour his attempt, since
he had completed the job before anyone suspected what
he was going to do. You say I prompted him. So presumably Milo was not the sort of man who could perform a
patriotic action without a prompter! I celebrated the
deed when it was done, you point out. But when the
whole nation was rejoicing, why should I be the only
mourner? Certainly, the inquiry into Clodius's death was
not very judiciously designed. For when an established

legal procedure for murder was available, the creation of a new law to deal with the case was pointless. Anyway, that is what was done, and the inquiry took its course. At the time, when the matter was under active consideration, no one brought this charge against me. It remained for you to perpetrate the fabrication after all these years!

Your next impudent accusation – made at considerable length – is that I was responsible for alienating Pompey from Caesar, and that by so doing I caused the Civil War. Your mistake in saying this is not wholly factual, but chronological; and this is a significant point. It is true that, during the consulship of the admirable Marcus Calpurnius Bibulus, I made every possible attempt to separate Pompey from Caesar. But Caesar was more successful: for he alienated Pompey from me. And when Pompey had wholeheartedly joined Caesar, how could I endeavour to set them apart? I should have been foolish to hope for such a thing – and impertinent to attempt persuasion. Yet there were two occasions on which I advised Pompey against Caesar. Blame me for them, if you can. First, I advised him not to renew Caesar's five-year term in Gaul; secondly, I urged him not to allow Caesar's candidature for the consulship *in absentia*. If I had been successful on either occasion, our present miseries would never have befallen us.

But instead Pompey made a present to Caesar of all his own resources, and all the resources of Rome. Only then did he belatedly begin to understand what I had foreseen long before. But by that time I had also come to realize that a criminal attack on our country was imminent. That is why, from then onward, I never ceased to urge peace, harmony, and arrangement. Many people knew what I was saying: 'If only, Pompey, you had either avoided joining Caesar or avoided breaking with him! Your strength of character demanded the former course, and your wisdom the latter!' That, Antony, was the advice I consistently gave in regard to Pompey and the crisis of our Republic. If this advice had prevailed, the Republic would still be flourishing: but you would not be, for your scandalous, down-at-heels, infamous behaviour would have brought you down.

However, these are old stories. Your new story is this: I was responsible for the killing of Caesar. Now, Senators, I am afraid I may look guilty, at this point, of a deplorable offence: namely the production, in a case against myself, of a sham prosecutor – a man who will load me with compliments whether I am entitled to them or not. For among the company who did that most glorious of deeds, my name was never once heard. Yet not a name among them remained secret. Secret, do I say? Every one of them was instantly known far and wide! It was much more likely, believe me, that men should have boasted of complicity, though they had nothing to do with the deed, than that having been accomplices they should have desired to conceal the fact. There were quite a number of them; some obscure, some youthful – not the sort of people who would keep anyone's identity quiet. So, if I had been involved, how on earth could my participation have remained unknown?

Besides – if we really need to assume that the prime movers in that operation needed prompting to free their country! – was it for me to inspire the two Brutuses?

Every day, in their own homes, each of them had the statue of Lucius Junius Brutus to gaze upon – and one of them had Gaius Servilius Ahala as well. These living Brutuses, with these ancestors, needed no outside advisers from other houses: they had advisers ready to hand within their own homes. Gaius Cassius Longinus, too, belongs to a clan incapable of tolerating not only autocracy but even excessive power in any single individual. Yet apparently he needed me as his instigator! On the contrary, even before his present distinguished associates were available, Cassius had proposed to perform this same task in Cilicia at the mouth of the Cydnus, if only Caesar, after deciding to moor his ships on one bank of the river, had not moored them on the other instead. And then again, when the recovery of freedom was at stake, what need had Gnaeus Domitius Ahenobarbus of me to inspire him? Inspiration enough for Domitius was the memory of how his noble father and his uncle had died – and how he himself had been deprived of his rights as a citizen. As for Gaius Trebonius, far from persuading him, I should not even have ventured to advise him – so close were his ties with Caesar. The existence of those ties increases the debt of gratitude which our country owes Trebonius: for one man's friendship seemed to him of less importance than the freedom of the Roman people – he could have shared autocracy, but he preferred to strike it down. Or was I Lucius Tillius Cimber's counsellor? No, my admiration for him after he had done the deed was a great deal stronger than my confidence, beforehand, that he would do it; I admired him all the more because he disregarded the personal favours he had received: he thought only of Rome. And then the two Serviliuses – whether to call them Cascas* or Ahalas I do not know. Do you suppose they needed my advice to urge them on? They had their love for their country. To enumerate all the rest would take too long; it reflects great credit on themselves, and great glory on Rome, that they were so many!

But remember, please, how this astute man demonstrated my complicity. 'When Caesar had been killed,' said he, 'Brutus immediately brandished aloft his bloodstained dagger and called out Cicero's name, congratulating him on the recovery of national freedom.' But this choice of myself, above all others – why must it indicate my foreknowledge? Consider instead whether the reason why Brutus called upon me was not this. The deed which he had done resembled the deeds which I had done myself: that is why he singled me out – to proclaim that he had modelled himself on me.

What a fool you are, Antony. Do you not understand this? If wanting Caesar to be killed (as you complain that I did) is a crime, then it is also criminal to have rejoiced when he was dead. For between the man who advises an action and the man who approves when it is done there is not the slightest difference. Whether I wished the deed to be performed or am glad after its performance, is wholly immaterial. Yet, with the exception of the men who wanted to make an autocratic monarch of him, all were willing for this to happen – or were glad when it

---

* Publius Servilius Casca, who struck the first blow against Caesar, and his brother Gaius.

had happened. So everyone is guilty! For every decent person, in so far as he had any say in the matter, killed Caesar! Plans, courage, opportunities were in some cases lacking; but the desire nobody lacked.

Just listen to the fatuity of this man – this sheep, rather. Here were his words: 'Brutus, whose name I mention with all respect, called out Cicero's name while he was holding the bloodstained dagger: from which you must understand that Cicero was an accomplice.' So, just because you suspect that I suspected something you call me a criminal, yet the man who brandished a dripping dagger is mentioned by you 'with all respect'! Very well, use this imbecile language if you must; and your actions and opinions are even more brainless. In the end, Consul, you will have to make up your mind! You must pronounce your final judgement on the cause of the Brutuses, Cassius, Gnaeus Domitius Ahenobarbus, Gaius Trebonius, and the rest. Sleep off your hangover – breathe it out. Perhaps a torch might be administered, to sting you out of your snoring over this far from unimportant matter. Will you never understand that you *must* decide which description to apply to the men who did that deed: are they murderers or are they the restorers of national freedom?

Concentrate, please – just for a little. Try to make your brain work for a moment as if you were sober. I confess I am their friend – you prefer to call me their associate. And yet even I refuse to see any compromise solution. If these men are not liberators of the Roman people and saviours of the state, then even I assert that they are worse than assassins, worse than murderers.

Indeed, on the assumption that even the murder of one's own father is less horrible than to kill the father of one's country, even parricides are better than they are.

Well, then, you wise and thoughtful man, what do you say to this: if they are parricides, why, in the Senate and Assembly, do you refer to them with respect? You will also have to explain why you yourself proposed Marcus Brutus's exemption from the laws* when he remained outside the city for more than ten days; why, at the Games of Apollo, he received such a complimentary reception; and why he and Cassius were given provincial commands, and supernumerary quaestors and legates were assigned to them for the purpose. This was all your doing! So evidently you do not regard them as murderers. It follows – since no compromise is possible – that you must regard them as liberators. What is the matter? I am not embarrassing you, am I? For I doubt if you are quite competent to grasp the sort of dilemma in which this places you. Anyway, what my conclusion amounts to is this: by not regarding Brutus and the rest as criminals, you have automatically proclaimed that they deserve the most glorious rewards.

So I must re-design my speech. I shall write to these men and say that, if anyone asks whether your charge against me is true, they must offer no denials. For, if I was their accomplice and they conceal the fact, I am afraid this may discredit them; whereas if I was invited to join them and refused, this will reflect the gravest

---

* As city-praetor he was not allowed to be away from Rome for more than ten nights.

discredit on me. For heaven will bear witness that Rome – that any nation throughout the whole world – has never seen a greater act than theirs! There has never been an achievement more glorious – more greatly deserving of renown for all eternity. So if you pen me in a Trojan horse of complicity with the chief partners in that deed, I do not protest. Thank you, I say – whatever your motives. For where so outstanding an action is concerned, I account the unpopularity, which you hope to unload upon me, as nothing beside the glory.

You have driven these men away and expelled them, you boast. Yet they are blessed beyond measure. There is no place in the world too deserted and too barbarous to welcome them and delight in their presence. All people on earth, however uncivilized, are capable of understanding that life could offer no more outstanding happiness than a sight of these men. Writers will continue, for generation after generation throughout time everlasting, to immortalize the glory of their achievement.

Enrol me among such heroes, I beg of you! Though I am afraid that one thing may not be to your liking. If I had been among their number I should have freed our country not only from the autocrat but from the autocracy. For if, as you assert, I had been the author of the work, believe me, I should not have been satisfied to finish only one act: I should have completed the play!*

If it is a crime to have wanted Caesar to be put to death, consider your own situation, Antony. Everyone

* i.e. killed Antony too.

44

knows that at Narbo you formed a similar plan with Gaius Trebonius: it was because of this plot, while Caesar was being killed, that we saw Trebonius taking you aside. You see – my intentions to you are friendly. I am praising you for the good intention you once had! For not having reported the plot, I thank you; for not having carried it out, I excuse you. That task needed a man.

But suppose that someone prosecutes you; that he applies the test of the jurist Lucius Cassius Longinus: 'who benefited thereby?'. Then you will have to take care, for you might be implicated. True, you used to observe, once upon a time, that such an act would benefit all who were unwilling to be slaves. Nevertheless, whom did its performance benefit most of all? Yourself! You, who, far from being a slave, are an autocratic ruler: you, who employed the treasure in the Temple of Ops to wipe off your gigantic debts, who after manipulating these same account-books squandered countless sums, who transferred enormous possessions from Caesar's house to your own. What an immensely profitable output of fake memoranda and forged handwritings your home produces! The place is a forger's workshop, a black market: whole properties and cities, mass exemptions from tribute and taxation are the wares of its truly scandalous trade.

Nothing short of Caesar's death could have rescued you from your debtor's ruin. You look rather worried. Are you secretly nervous that you may be implicated? No, I can set your fears at rest: no one will ever believe such a thing of you. You are not the man to perform a patriotic act. Our country has great men, and they did that noble deed. I do not say you took part. I only say you were glad.

Now I have answered your most serious accusations. Well, I must reply to the others. You have complained about my presence in Pompey's camp, and about my conduct throughout that period. True, at that time – and I have said this before – if my advice and authority had prevailed, you would be a poor man today, and we should be free; and our country would not have lost so many armies and commanders. For when I foresaw what has now happened, I confess that I mourned as sadly as all other good citizens, if they had possessed my foresight, would likewise have mourned. I grieved, Senators, I grieved that our Republic, which your and my counsels had once preserved, was moving towards rapid annihilation. In such circumstances I was not uneducated and ignorant enough to be overcome by fears whether I personally should survive. For my life, while it was still mine, was full of anguish; whereas its loss would mean an end of all troubles. But I wanted life to remain for the magnificent men who were Rome's glory – all those who have served as consul and praetor, the fine Senators, the flower and promise of our nobility, the armies of good Romans. So for me any peace that could unite our citizens seemed preferable to a war that tore them apart. And indeed, however hard the circumstances of peace, if those men were only living today, at least the Republic would still be with us.

If this view of mine had prevailed, and if the very men whose lives I sought to preserve had not, in their military over-optimism, set themselves against me, one of many results would certainly be this: you would never still be in the Senate. You would not even be at Rome!

You object that my speech alienated Pompey from me. That is absurd. He had more affection for me than for anyone. There was no one in the world whom he talked to and consulted more often. Indeed it was a splendid thing that two men with so widely differing views on government policy should remain such close friends. Each of us knew, equally well, the thoughts and opinions of the other. My first concern was to keep our fellow-Romans alive: by so doing, we could give ourselves time to think later on about their civic rights. Pompey, on the other hand, was preoccupied with their rights in the immediate present. Nevertheless, our disagreement was tolerable – the more so because we both concentrated on our own specific objectives.

But what Pompey, with his outstanding and almost superhuman gifts, thought about myself is well known to those who accompanied him on his retreat from Pharsalus to Paphos. He never mentioned my name except in complimentary terms and with an abundance of friendly regrets that we were not together. He also admitted that, whereas his had been the higher hopes, the more accurate prophet had been myself. But how can you have the effrontery to taunt me with Pompey, when you have to admit that I was his friend: whereas you, on the other hand, were the purchaser of his confiscated property!

However, let us say no more about that war – in which you fared only too well. Nor have I any answer to give you about the jokes which you say I made while

I was in camp. Life was certainly anxious there. Yet however grim circumstances are, human beings, if they really are human, occasionally relax. Antony criticizes my gloom, and he criticizes my jokes! Which proves that I showed moderation in both.

No one left me any legacies,* you said. I only wish that the charge were justified, for then more of my friends and relations would be alive today. But I wonder how that idea came into your mind. For men have made me bequests amounting to more than twenty million sesterces. True, I admit that in this respect you have been more fortunate than I have. For all who have made me their heirs have been my friends. That has been their way of soothing my grief with some mitigating benefit – if it could be regarded as such. But you inherited from Lucius Rubrius Casinas: whom you had never seen! He must indeed have loved you dearly, seeing that you do not even know whether he was black or white. He passed over in your favour the sons of that very worthy knight, his friend Quintus Fufius. Rubrius had constantly announced, in public, that Fufius's son was to be his heir. And yet he did not even mention him in his will! Instead, you were the man he made his heir – you whom he had never seen or, at any rate, had never spoken to. And tell me this, please, if it is not too much trouble: what did your other benefactor Lucius Turselius look like? How tall was he, where did he come from, what was his tribe? 'I know nothing,' you will answer, 'except what

* It was regarded as a slight not to be mentioned in a friend's will. Lawyers, who were not allowed to accept fees, particularly expected this sort of reward.

properties he owned.' Was that sufficient cause for him to disinherit his brother and make you his heir? But there were many others too, equally remote from any connexion with him, from whom Antony grabbed huge sums of money, ejecting the true heirs, and behaving as if he himself were the inheritor.

And there is another reason too why I am surprised, particularly surprised, that you should have had the impudence even to mention matters of inheritance. For you did not come into your own father's property!

Fool! Were these the arguments you were trying to hunt out when you spent day after day in another man's country house, practising oratory? Though your oratorical practice, as your closest friends point out, is intended to work off your hangovers rather than to sharpen your brain, you have facetiously appointed a teacher of oratory – the appointment carried by the supporting votes of your fellow-drinkers – and you have allowed the man to speak against you in any way he likes. He is certainly an amusing enough fellow. But, since you and your friends are his targets, he cannot complain of any lack of material!

Note the contrast between yourself and your grandfather. He, with deliberation, produced arguments relevant to his case; you just pour out irrelevancies. And yet what a salary your teacher of rhetoric has drawn from you. Listen to this, Senators: take note of the wounds inflicted upon our nation. To this elocution trainer – Sextus Clodius – he handed over 1,250 acres of land, tax-free. You made the people of Rome defray this enormous charge, Antony, with no other result than to make you learn to be the idiot that you are. You unprincipled rogue! Was this one of the directions you found in Caesar's notebooks? However, about this estate at Leontini I will say something later; also about other properties in Campania – all of them lands which Antony has wrenched from Rome, and polluted by the utterly degraded characters of the men to whom he has given them.

I have said enough in answer to his charges. Now some attention must be given to our moralist and reformer himself. However, I do not propose to tell the whole story at once: so that if I have to return to the fray, I shall not need to repeat myself. In view of the extraordinary quantity of his crimes and vices, that presents no difficulty.

Would you like us to consider your behaviour from boyhood onwards, Antony? I think so. Let us begin then at the beginning. Your bankruptcy, in early adolescence – do you remember that? Your father's fault, you will say. Certainly; and what a truly filial self-defence! But it was typical of your impudence to go to the theatre and sit in one of the fourteen rows reserved for knights, when the Roscian Law assigned special seats for bankrupts – and meant this to apply whether it was bad luck or bad conduct had caused the bankruptcy. Then you graduated to man's clothing – or rather it was woman's as far as you were concerned. At first you were just a public prostitute, with a fixed price: quite a high one, too. But very soon Curio intervened and took you off the streets, promoting you, one might say, to wifely status, and making a sound, steady, married woman of you. No boy bought for sensual purposes was ever so completely in his master's power as you were in Curio's. On countless occasions his father threw you out of the house. He even stationed guards to keep you out! Nevertheless, helped by nocturnal darkness, urged on by sensuality, compelled by the promised fee – in, through the roof, you climbed.

The household found these repulsive goings on completely unendurable. I wonder if you realize that I have a very thorough knowledge of what I am speaking about. Cast your mind back to the time when Curio's father lay weeping in his bed. The son, likewise in tears, threw himself at my feet and begged me to help you – and to defend himself against a demand, which he expected from his own father, for six million sesterces. The young man loved you so passionately that he swore he would leave the country because he could not bear to be kept apart from you. In those days, within that renowned family, there were troubles without number which I helped to mitigate – or rather, brought to an end altogether. I persuaded the father to pay his son's debts. I persuaded him to sacrifice part of his property to restore the position of this young man, whose promise of brain and character was so brilliant. But I also persuaded him to use all his legal authority as a father to prevent Curio from associating with you or even meeting you. When you remembered all these interventions of mine, only one thing can have given you the nerve to provoke and abuse me in the way you have, and that is your reliance on the brute force of arms: the weapons which we see in the Senate today.

But about Antony's degradations and sex-crimes that is as far as I will go. For there are some things which it would be indecent for me to describe. As far as free speaking goes you have the advantage of me! – since you have done things which a respectable opponent cannot even mention. So instead I will now turn briefly to the remaining portion of this man's life. For our thoughts will naturally run on to what he did during the national miseries of the Civil War – and what he is doing today. You know those things, Senators, as well as I do, and indeed much better. Yet continue, I beg of you, to listen to them carefully. For in such cases knowledge about events is not enough. There is also need to be reminded of them: only thus will they be fully felt.

However, since I must allow myself time to reach the end of these happenings, I must cut short the middle part of the story. Well, Antony now recounts his kindnesses towards me. All the same, when Publius Clodius was tribune, the two men were intimate friends. Antony was the firebrand who started all Clodius's fires. Indeed, one of his projects – he knows very well which one I mean – was actually located in Clodius's home. Then Antony went to Alexandria: in defiance of the Senate, and of patriotism, and of the will of heaven. But he was under a man with whom he could do no wrong – Aulus Gabinius. Then consider the nature and circumstances of Antony's return. Before he came home, he went from Egypt to farthest Gaul. Home, did I say? At that time, other men still possessed homes: but you, Antony, had none at all. Home? You had no piece of ground of your own in the whole world, except at Misenum; and that you only shared with partners, as though it were a company affair like the Sisapo mines.

From Gaul you came to stand for the quaestorship. On that occasion, I dare you to claim that you went to your father before you came to me! I had already received a letter from Caesar asking me to accept your excuses; so I did not even allow you to thank me. After that, you treated me with respect, and I helped you in your candidature for the quaestorship. That was the time when, with the approval of Rome, you tried to kill Publius Clodius. Now, though this was entirely your own idea, and owed nothing to my initiative, nevertheless you proclaimed the conviction that only his murder could ever repay me for the injuries I had suffered from you. This makes me wonder why you say Titus Annius Milo killed Clodius on my instigation. For, when you spontaneously proposed to me that you should perform the same action, I had given you no encouragement. If you went through with the deed, I wanted you yourself, and not my influence upon you, to have the glory.

Well, you became quaestor; and instantly – without benefit of Senate's decree, drawing of lots, or legal sanction – you ran off to Caesar. For that seemed to you the only place on earth where destitution, debt, and crime could find shelter: the only refuge for ruined men. There, through Caesar's generosity and your own looting, you reimbursed your losses – if you can call it reimbursement when you immediately squander what you have embezzled! So then, beggared again, you hastened to apply

for a tribuneship. Your aim in acquiring it, presumably,
was to model yourself on your lover.

Now listen, I beg you, Senators, I do not mean to the
personal and domestic scandals created by Antony's disgusting improprieties, but to the evil, godless way in
which he has undermined us all, and our fortunes, and our
whole country. At the root of all our disasters you will
find his wickedness. When Lucius Cornelius Lentulus
Crus and Gaius Claudius Marcellus became consuls on
the first of January, the Republican government was
tottering and on the verge of collapse. You, members of
the Senate, wanted to support the government; you also
desired to meet the wishes of Caesar himself, if he was
in his right mind. Yet Antony had sold and subjected his
tribuneship to another man, and he exploited the office
for your obstruction. That is to say, to the axe which
had struck down many men for lesser crimes he had the
audacity to expose his own neck. In those days the Senate
was still its own master; those honourable members who
are now dead were still among its number. That Senate,
Antony, employed for your censure the decree reserved,
by ancestral custom, for Roman citizens who are the
enemies of Rome. And yet, as audience for your criti-
cisms of me, you have the impertinence to select the
Senate – that very body which pronounced me to be its
saviour, and you the enemy of the state!

Your criminal action at that time has not been mentioned lately; but what you did has not been forgotten.
So long as there are human beings in the world, so long
as the name of Rome remains upon the earth – and
that means everlastingly, barring destructive action by

yourself – that pestilential veto* of yours will be remembered. In the Senate's proceedings there had not been the slightest sign of bias or impetuosity. Yet you, a single young man, imposed your veto, and thus prevented the entire Senatorial Order from passing a measure on which the safety of our nation depended. And this you did not once, but repeatedly. Furthermore, you rejected all efforts to open negotiations with you about upholding the authority of this House. Yet the matter at stake was nothing less than your itch to plunge the whole country into anarchy and desolation. The pleas of the nation's leaders, the warnings of your elders, a crowded Senate, none of them sufficed to deter you from this measure you had been bribed and bought into proposing.

Next, therefore, after many attempts to dissuade you, there was no alternative; you had to be dealt the blow which few had received before – and which none had survived. So this Senatorial Order directed the consuls, and other powers and authorities, to take up arms against you. You only escaped those arms by sheltering behind Caesar's.

Caesar's intentions were wholly revolutionary. But the man who gave him his principal excuse for attacking his country was yourself. For that was the only pretext he claimed, the only reason he put forward for his maniacal decision and action: he quoted the Senate's

---

* On 2 January 49 BC, Antony and another tribune had vetoed a proposal in the Senate that unless Caesar disbanded his army before a named date he should be declared a public enemy. Caesar crossed the Rubicon eight days later.

disregard of a veto, its abolition of a tribune's entitlement, its encroachment on Antony's rights. I say nothing of the falsity and frivolity of these charges – though no man can possibly be justified in taking up arms against his own nation. But I am not speaking of Caesar. You, Antony, were the man who provided the pretext for this most catastrophic of wars: you cannot deny it.

If what I am now going to say is known to you already, then your fate is sad indeed: and sadder still if it is not. Now, there exist written records, to be recollected without possibility of oblivion by remotest posterity until the end of time, proving that these things happened. That the consuls were expelled from Italy; that they were accompanied by the man whose glory illuminated our nation – Pompey; that all former consuls whose health enabled them to share in that disastrous retreat, all praetors and ex-praetors, tribunes of the people, a great part of the Senate, the flower of our young manhood, in a word all the components of the entire Roman state, were uprooted and driven from their homes.

Just as seeds are the origins of trees and plants, so, with equal certainty, you were the seed of that most grievous war. Senators, you are mourning three armies of Roman soldiers slain in battle: Antony killed them. You are sorrowing for great men of Rome: Antony robbed you of them. The authority of your Order has been destroyed: Antony destroyed it. For every evil which we have seen since that time – and what evils have we not seen? – he is responsible. There can be no other conclusion. He has been our Helen of Troy! He has brought upon our country war, and pestilence, and annihilation.

The rest of his tribuneship resembled the beginning. Of all the misdeeds which the Senate, while the Republic was still with us, had rendered impossible there was not one which he left undone. And note the crimes within his crime. Though he rehabilitated many who were in trouble, there was no mention of his uncle among them. But if he was severe, why was he not severe to everyone? and if merciful, why not merciful to his own kinsmen?

Among those whose civil rights he restored I will only mention Licinius Lenticula, his fellow-dicer – a man convicted for gambling. I can only suppose Antony protested that his partner at the tables must not be a convict! But his real aim was to utilize the law cancelling Lenticula's sentence as a cloak for the cancellation of his own gaming debts. Now, Antony, what reasons justifying his reinstatement did you quote to the people of Rome? The normal sort of argument would run like this: that Lenticula had been absent when the prosecution was instituted against him; that the case went undefended, that the law provided no judicial procedure to deal with dicing, that armed violence had been used to procure his downfall, or as a final objection what was said in your uncle's case – that the court's decision had been influenced by bribery. But not at all. Those were not your excuses. What you urged was that Lenticula was a good man, useful to his country. Well, that was irrelevant. All the same, I should excuse you on that count if your plea were only true, for the mere fact of having been convicted is of no great importance. But there is not a word of truth in it. Lenticula has been condemned under the law which relates to dicing: he is the sort of person who would not hesitate to throw dice in the Forum itself – a thoroughly criminal type. The man who can restore the rights of such a ruffian reveals a great deal about his own character.

Then consider another aspect of Antony's tribuneship. When Caesar, on his way to Spain, had given him Italy to trample upon, the journeys Antony made and the towns he visited are well worth looking into. I realize I am speaking of matters which are thoroughly well known and widely talked about. I am also aware that the events of which I am, and shall be, speaking are better known to anyone who was in Italy at that time than to myself who was absent. Nevertheless, although what I tell you will undoubtedly fall short of what you know already, allow me to recall certain particulars.

For never, anywhere in the world, have there been stories of such depraved and discreditable misconduct. He travelled about in a lady's carriage, did this tribune of the people. In front of him marched attendants crowned with laurel-wreaths. Among them, carried in an open litter, went an actress. The respectable citizens of the country towns, compelled to come and meet him, greeted her, not by her well-known stage name, but as Volumnia. Next followed a repulsive collection of his friends: a four-wheeler full of procurers. Only then came his neglected mother, following, like a mother-in-law, her debauched son's mistress. Poor woman! Her capacity for child-bearing has indeed been catastrophic. In such fashion a wide variety of country towns, indeed the whole of Italy, was branded by Antony with the marks of his degraded behaviour.

To censure his other actions, Senators, is difficult and delicate. He fought in the war. He wallowed in the blood of Romans who were in every way his opposites. He was fortunate, if there can ever be good fortune in criminality. But since we do not want to offend the old soldiers – though the soldiers' case and yours, Antony, are wholly unlike (they followed their leader, you went to seek him out) – nevertheless I shall give you no opportunity to incite them against me. For concerning the character of the war I shall say nothing.

From Thessaly to Brundisium you returned as conqueror with your legions. At Brundisium you refrained from killing me. How very kind of you! For you could have killed me, I admit. Though the men who were with you at that time unanimously maintained I must be spared. For even your own legionaries revered me: so great is man's love for their country, which they remembered that I had saved. However, let us concede that you gave me as a present what you did not take away from me; you did not deprive me of my life, which I therefore retain as a gift from yourself. After hearing all your insults I nearly forgot my gratitude, though not quite. And there was something particularly impudent about your abuse, because you knew how I would be able to retaliate!

Arrival at Brundisium for you meant envelopment in the embraces of your little actress. Well, is that a lie? It is distressing, is it not, to be unable to deny something that is disreputable to admit. But if the townsmen caused you to feel no shame, did not your own veteran army? For every single soldier who was at Brundisium saw her. Every one of them knew she had come all those days' journey to congratulate you: every man grieved to have found out so late in the day the worthlessness of the leader he had followed.

Again you toured Italy, with this actress by your side. In the communities through which you passed, amid scenes of brutality and misery, you planted your soldiers as settlers. At Rome you cut a deplorable figure as a robber of gold and silver – and of wine. As a climax, unknown to Caesar (who was at Alexandria), Caesar's friends were kind enough to make Antony his Master of Horse. At that juncture he felt entitled to live with Hippias; and to hand over race-horses, intended for the national games, to another actor Sergius. At that time Antony had chosen to live, not in the house which he so discreditably retains now, but in Marcus Pupius Piso's home. His decrees, his looting, his legacies inherited and grabbed I will pass over in silence. Need compelled him: he did not know which way to turn. Those substantial inheritances from Lucius Rubrius Casinas and Lucius Turselius had not yet come to him; not yet had he become the unexpected 'heir' to Pompey, and many more. He had nothing except what he could plunder; he was obliged to live like a bandit.

But about these examples of the tougher sorts of rascality, I shall speak no more. Let us turn instead to meaner kinds of misbehaviour. With those jaws of yours, and those lungs, and that gladiatorial strength, you drank so much wine at Hippias's wedding, Antony, that on the next day you had to be sick in full view of the people of Rome. It was a disgusting sight; even to hear what happened is disgusting. If you had behaved like that at a private dinner party, among those outsize drinking cups of yours, everyone would have regarded it as disgraceful enough. But here, in the Assembly of the Roman People, was a man holding public office, a Master of the Horse – from whom even a belch would have been unseemly – flooding his own lap and the whole platform with the gobbets of wine-reeking food he had vomited up. He admits that this was one of his filthier actions: let us now return to his grander misdeeds.

Well, Caesar returned from Alexandria, a fortunate man – as he seemed to himself at least: though in my view no one who brings misfortune upon his country can be called fortunate. The spear was set up before the temple of Jupiter Stator; and Pompey's property – the very thought brings unhappiness! for even when the tears no longer flow the sorrow remains deeply fixed in my heart – Pompey's property, I say, was subjected to the pitiless voice of the auctioneer.

On that single occasion the nation forgot its slavery, and mourned. Men felt slaves, because fear gripped them all, yet, even so, the people of Rome lamented freely enough. Every man waited to see if there would be some depraved madman, repulsive to heaven and humanity, who would dare to take part in that criminal auction. Though some of the men round that spear would have stopped at nothing else, no one had audacity enough for this – no one except Antony alone! One person, only one, was shameless enough to perpetrate the act which all others, however great their effrontery, had shunned in horror. But, Antony, were you too totally witless – or is not insanity the appropriate word? – to realize this: that in your station of life to become a purchaser of confiscated property, and of Pompey's property at that, would earn you the curses and loathing of the Roman people, the detestation of all gods and all human beings, now and for evermore? And then, think of the arrogance with which this debauchee took instant possession of the estate! The estate of a man who through his valour had made Rome more greatly feared, and by his justice had made her more greatly loved, by all the other nations upon earth.

So, abruptly seizing that great man's property, Antony wallowed in its midst. In his mighty satisfaction he gloated, like the character in a play who was poor and has suddenly become rich. But as some poet wrote, 'ill-gotten gains will soon be squandered'. And the unbe-lievable – almost miraculous – fact is that he squandered Pompey's substantial fortune, not in a few months, but in a few days! In that house there were large quantities of wine, heavy pieces of the finest silver-ware, costly robes, ample and elegant furniture – all the splendid and abundant property of a man who, though not luxurious, had none the less been nobly endowed with possessions. Of these, within a few days, nothing was left! Charybdis, if she ever existed, was but a single animal. I swear that such a number of objects so widely scattered in so great a variety of places could hardly have been swallowed up, at such a speed, by the Ocean itself.

Nothing was locked up, nothing sealed, nothing listed.

Whole store-rooms were disposed of as gifts, to unmitigated scoundrels. Actors and actresses grabbed everything they wanted. The place was packed with gamblers, crammed with inebriates. For days on end, in many parts of the house, the orgies of drinking went on and on. Gaming losses piled up; Antony's good luck did not always hold. On view were the richly worked counterpanes which had belonged to Pompey – now they were in the garrets of slaves, and on their beds!

So let it not surprise you that these riches were consumed with such speed. A profligacy so boundless as Antony's could have rapidly devoured not just a single man's patrimony, even one so abundant as Pompey's, but whole cities and whole kingdoms. And then the mansion and the parks that he took over! Your impudence, Antony, was preposterous. How could you have the effrontery to enter that house, to pass its most sacred threshold, to let the household gods of such an abode see you flaunting your degraded features? This was a home which no one, for many days and months, could gaze upon or pass by without weeping. As you linger on within its rooms, are you not overcome with shame?

You are brainless, I know: yet surely, even so, none of the things that are there can bring you enjoyment. When you look at those beaks of ships* in the hall, you cannot possibly imagine that the house you are entering is your own! That would be out of the question. For all your lack of sense and sensibility, still you are aware of what you yourself are, you know your own people and

---

* Captured by Pompey in his campaign against the pirates in 67 BC.

possessions. So I do not believe that, waking or sleeping, you can ever feel easy in your mind. Drink-sodden and demented though you are, the appearance in your dreams of that great man must surely rouse you in terror; and when you are awake, too, his recurring image must unhinge your mind still further.

I pity the very walls and roof of that house. For never before had the place witnessed anything but strict propriety – fine, high-minded tradition and virtue. As you know very well, Senators, Pompey was as praiseworthy in his domestic as in his international dealings; as admirable in his home life as in public affairs he was renowned. Yet nowadays, in his home, every dining-room is a taproom, every bedroom a brothel. Antony may deny this nowadays. Be tactful; do not investigate! For he has become economical. He has told that actress of his to gather up her own property and hand back his keys, as the Twelve Tables ordain – and he has driven her out. What a reputable citizen! What solid respectability! Here is the most honourable action of his whole life; he has divorced his actress.

How he harps on the phrase: 'I, the consul Antony.' That amounts to saying, 'I, the consul, debauchee', or 'I, the consul, criminal'. For that is the significance of 'Antony'. If there were any dignity in the name, I presume that your grandfather, too, would sometimes have called himself 'the consul, Antony'. But he never did. So would your uncle, who was my colleague. Or has there been no Antony but yourself?

However, I pass over these offences, for they had no direct connexion with the part you played in ruining our country. I return to the latter – to the Civil War, which owed its birth, its rise, and its performance to yourself. True, your role in the war was insignificant. That was because you were frightened, or rather preoccupied with your sexual interests. But you had tasted Roman blood; indeed you had drunk deeply of it. At Pharsalus you were in the front rank. It was you who killed that fine nobleman, Lucius Domitius Ahenobarbus – as well as many others, fugitives from the battle-field. Caesar would perhaps have spared them, as he spared others. But you, on the other hand, hunted them down for your slaughter.

However, after these grand and glorious achievements, the war was still by no means ended. So why did you not follow Caesar to Africa? And then, when Caesar had returned from Africa, let us note the position and rank which he assigned to you. As general he had made you quaestor, when he was dictator you had become his Master of the Horse. You had begun the war. Every atrocity had been instigated by yourself; in each successive robbery you had been his associate. We have it on your own authority that his will adopted you as his son.* Yet what did he now do? He took action against you – the sums you owed for the house, and for its parks and the other property you acquired in the auction, were all demanded back from you by Caesar.

Your initial reply was vigorous enough: and, I admit – for I do not want to seem prejudiced against you –

---

* It had been a blow for Antony when Caesar's published will reserved this distinction for Octavian, appointing Antony as one of the secondary heirs only.

reasonably fair and just. 'So Caesar claims money from me? Could I not just as reasonably claim money from him – or did he win the war without my help? No: nor could he have. It was I who provided him with the pretext for the Civil War, I who proposed those subversive laws, who forcibly resisted not merely the Roman people's consuls and generals, but the entire Senate and Roman people and the gods and altars and homes of our fathers – indeed Rome itself. Caesar did not conquer for himself alone; why should those who shared the work not share the plunder too?' Reasonable enough. But reason was beside the point, for Caesar was the stronger. So he silenced you, and you and your guarantors received a visit from his soldiers.

And then, suddenly, out came that spectacular list of yours. Everyone laughed at the size of the list – at the varied and extensive catalogue of possessions, none of which (except a part of the Misenum property) the seller could call his own. But the auction itself was a melancholy sight. Few of Pompey's robes were now to be seen, and even they were covered with stains; a certain amount of his silver plate appeared in battered condition; and there were some seedy-looking slaves. So the remains were meagre enough. If nothing at all had survived, our grief would have been less.

However, the heirs of Lucius Rubrius Casinas pre-vented the auction, and they were backed by a decree from Caesar. Antony, the wild spender, was embarrassed – he had nowhere to turn. And that was the precise moment of the arrest in Caesar's house (so the report went) of an assassin, dagger in hand – sent by you,

Antony: and Caesar charged you openly with this in the Senate. Next, however, after allowing you a few days for payment – since you were so poor – he departed for Spain. Even then you did not follow him. So early a retirement, for so good a gladiator? A man who showed such timidity in standing up for his party (and that means standing up for himself) need surely inspire no fear in others!

In the end, some time afterwards, Antony did leave for Spain. But he proved unable to reach that country safely, he maintains. Then how did Publius Cornelius Dolabella get there? Either you ought not to have backed the cause you did, Antony, or, having done so, you ought to have stood up for your side to the end. Three times Caesar fought against his fellow-citizens: in Thessaly, in Africa, and in Spain. Dolabella took part in all these campaigns; in the Spanish war he was wounded. If you want to know my view, I wish he had not been there. Yet however blameworthy his initial decision, at least he deserves praise for consistent adherence thereafter. But what about yourself? That was the time when Pompey's sons were fighting to make their way home – a matter, surely, which concerned all Caesar's partisans. In other words, Pompey's sons were struggling to recover the shrines of their household gods, their sacred hearth and home, and the guardian spirits of their family – all of which you had seized. When, in order to recover what was theirs by law, they were obliged to use force, who would most justly (though indeed among such grievous wrongs to speak of justice is impossible) – who, I say, would be their principal target? The answer is, yourself, the taker of their property. So it was your battle, was it not, that Dolabella had to fight in Spain: while you stayed at Narbo, vomiting over your hosts' tables.

And your return from Narbo! Antony actually wanted to know why *I* returned from my journey so suddenly. Now I have recently explained to the Senate the reasons for my return. I wanted, if I could, to be of service to the state even before the New Year. You ask how I returned. First, I arrived by daylight, not after dark. Secondly, I came in my boots and toga, not in Gallic sandals and a cloak. I see your eyes fixed upon me: in anger, it appears. But you ought, instead, to harbour friendly feelings if only you knew how ashamed I am – unlike yourself – of the depths to which you have fallen. Of all the offences that I have seen or heard of as committed by any single person this is the most deplorable. You, who claimed to have been Master of the Horse, who were standing for one of next year's consulships – or rather begging for one of them as a personal favour – off you went, in your Gallic sandals and mantle, speeding through the towns of Cisalpine Gaul: the towns in which, when we were candidates for consulships, we used to seek votes – in the days when these appointments went by votes and not by personal favour.

Note the frivolity of the man. When, at about three o'clock, he approached Rome and came to Red Rocks, he dived into a wretched little wine-shop, and, hiding there, drank and drank until evening. Then a two-wheeler took him rapidly into the city and he arrived at his house with his head veiled. 'Who are you?' said the porter. 'A messenger from Antony,' he replied. He was immediately taken to the lady for whose sake he had come, and he handed her a letter. As she read the contents, she wept; for it was amorously written – and the gist was that he had given up the actress and transferred all his love to this other lady. And as her weeping increased, this soft-hearted fellow could bear the sight no longer, but uncovered his head and threw his arms round her neck. Depraved character! No other epithet is adequate for this creature who plunged the city into terror by night, plunged Italy into a series of nerve-racking days, merely in order to make his sudden appearance before this woman. What a surprise this must have been to her: to see such behaviour from a male prostitute.

At home, then, you could lay claim to a love affair. But elsewhere there was an even nastier affair for you: to prevent Lucius Munatius Plancus from selling up your sureties. A tribune brought you before a public meeting, and you replied: 'I have come here on a matter concerning my private property.' This was regarded by everyone as an excellent joke.*

However, that is enough about trivialities; let us turn to more significant matters. When Caesar came back from Spain, you travelled a long way to meet him. You went quickly, and you returned quickly: Caesar could therefore note that, if not brave, you were at least energetic. Somehow or other you got on friendly terms with him again. Caesar was like that. He was extremely ready to offer his intimate friendship to anyone whom

---

* The joke was that Antony was notoriously impoverished, a disgrace according to Roman ideas.

he knew to be corrupt and unbalanced, penniless, and hopelessly in debt. In these respects your credentials were excellent. So he gave orders that you should be made consul – with himself, moreover, as your colleague. One can only feel sympathy with Publius Cornelius Dolabella, who had been urged to stand, brought forward, and then fobbed off. Everyone knows how deceitfully both of you treated Dolabella in this matter. Caesar induced him to be a candidate for the consulship, and then, after promising and virtually granting him election, blocked the proceedings and transferred the post to himself. And you supported this treachery.

The first of January arrived. We were made to attend the Senate. Dolabella attacked Antony – with much greater fullness and preparation than I do now. And heavens, the things that Antony himself said in his rage! Caesar indicated his intention, before his forthcoming departure for the east, of ordering that Dolabella should become consul in his own place. And yet they deny that the man who was always acting and speaking like that was a totalitarian monarch! Well, after Caesar had said that, this splendid augur Antony announced that his priesthood empowered him to employ the auspices in order to obstruct or invalidate the proceedings of the Assembly. And he declared that this is what he would do. But first note the man's unbelievable stupidity. For your priestly office of augur, Antony, was what you relied upon for entitlement to perform those actions. Yet, as consul alone, without the added possession of your augurship, your entitlement would still have been just as good. Indeed, was your consulship not actually a better qualification? For we augurs are only empowered to report omens, whereas the consuls and other state officials have the right actually to watch the heavens.

Very well, you bungled the matter through inexperience. We cannot expect good judgement from someone who is never sober. But just observe the man's impudence. Many months earlier he had declared in the Senate that he would either use the auspices to prevent the Assembly from meeting to elect Dolabella, or alternatively would act as he finally did. Now, who on earth can divine what flaws there are going to be in the auspices, except the man who has already formally set about watching the heavens? Which cannot legally be done during an election – and if anyone has been watching the heavens previously, he is obliged to make his report not after but before the election has begun. But Antony is as ignorant as he is shameless: the insolence his actions display is as unbounded as his ignorance of what an augur ought to do. And yet cast your minds back to his consulship, from that day onwards until the fifteenth of March. No servant was ever so humble and abject. He could do nothing himself; everything had to be begged for. You could see him poking his head into the back of his litter asking his colleague* for the favours Antony wanted to market.

So the day of Dolabella's election arrived. The right of the first vote is settled by lot; Antony said nothing. The result of this ballot was announced. He remained silent. The first class was called to vote, its vote

* Caesar, his fellow-consul.

announced; then the six centuries which voted next, then the second class – all this in a shorter time than it takes to tell the story. Then, when the proceedings were over, came our brilliant augur's announcement – you would say he was Gaius Laelius himself: 'the meeting is adjourned until another day'. What monstrous impudence! You had neither seen, nor understood, nor heard, any omen whatever. You did not even claim to have watched the heavens; you do not today. So the flaw in question was the one which you had foreseen and foretold as long ago as the first of January! In other words, you undoubtedly falsified the auspices. You employed religion to constrain an Assembly of the Roman People. You announced unfavourable omens, augur to augur, consul to consul: and you did so fraudulently. May the calamitous consequences fall not upon Rome, but upon your own head.

That is all I shall say, in case I should seem to be invalidating the actions of Dolabella – which must, at some time, be referred to our Board of Augurs. But mark the man's audacious arrogance. As long as it is your pleasure, Antony, the election of Dolabella as consul was irregular. Then you change your mind: the procedure in regard to the auspices had nothing wrong with it after all! If an augur's report in the terms you employed has no meaning, then admit that when you demanded an adjournment you were drunk. If, on the other hand, the words have any meaning at all, then I request you, as my fellow-augur, to tell me what their meaning is.

But I must make sure that this survey of Antony's numerous exploits does not by accident omit one outstandingly brilliant action. So let us turn to the festival of the Lupercalia. Look, Senators! He cannot hide his anxiety. Do you see how upset he looks – pale, and sweating? Never mind, so long as he is not sick, as he was in the Minucian Colonnade. How does he defend his scandalous behaviour at the Lupercalia? I should like to hear – and thereby learn the results of that generous fee and those lands at Leontini, which he gave his teacher of oratory.

Upon the dais on a golden chair, wearing a purple robe and a wreath, was seated your colleague. You mounted the dais. You went up to Caesar's chair – Lupercus though you were, you should have re-membered you were consul too – and you displayed a diadem. From all over the Forum there were groans. Where did the diadem come from? You had not just found one on the ground and picked it up. No, you had brought it from your own house! This was crime, deliberate and premeditated. Then you placed the dia-dem on his head: the people groaned. He took it off – and they applauded.

So, criminal, you were ready, alone among all that gathering, to propose that there should be a king and autocrat at Rome; to transform your fellow-consul into your lord and master; and to inflict upon the Roman people this ultimate test of its capacity to suffer and endure. You even tried to move him to pity – when you hurled yourself at his feet as a suppliant. What were you begging for? To become his slave? For yourself alone that would be a fitting plea, seeing that from boyhood onwards there was nothing which you had not allowed to be done to you. For your own person, adjustment to slavery was easy. But from ourselves, and from the people of Rome, you had no such mandate.

What glorious eloquence that was – when you made that speech with no clothes on! Offensive misbehaviour could go no further. Nothing could have been more thoroughly deserving of the severest possible punishment. Are you a slave, cowering in expectation of the lash? If you have any feelings at all, you must be feeling the lash now: and my account of these events must surely be drawing blood. Far be it from me to detract from the glory of our noble liberators. Yet such is my grief that I must speak out. Seeing that the man who rejected the diadem was killed, and was, by general consent, killed justly, it is appalling that the man who made him the offer should still be alive. In the public records, what is more, under the heading of the Lupercalia, he even caused the following entry to be made: 'At the bidding of the people, Antony, consul, offered Caesar, perpetual dictator, the kingship: Caesar refused.'

So I feel no surprise when you disturb the peace, when you shun Rome and the very daylight itself, when you drink with thieving riff-raff from early in one day until dawn of the next. For you, no refuge can be safe. Where could you possibly find a place in any community owning laws and lawcourts – since these are precisely what you have done your utmost to abolish and to replace by tyranny? Was this why Tarquin was expelled, why Spurius Cassius Vecellinus and Spurius Maelius and Marcus Manlius Capitolinus were slain: to allow Antony, centuries after they were dead, to commit the forbidden evil of setting up a king at Rome?

Let us return to the auspices, the subject on which Caesar intended to address the Senate on the fifteenth of March. Antony, I must ask you this: what would you then have said? You came here today (or so I heard) primed to rebut my assertion that the auspices – which unless declared invalid require scrupulous obedience – were employed by you in a fraudulent manner. However, that day's business was eliminated – by our national destiny. Did Caesar's death also eliminate your opinion concerning the auspices?

But now I have come to that time which I must discuss before the subject upon which I had embarked. On that glorious day, you fled panic-stricken – your criminal conscience certain of impending death. You slunk surreptitiously home. Men interested in your survival looked after you; for they hoped you would behave sanely. My prophecies of the future have always fallen upon deaf ears. Yet how completely right they have proved! On the Capitol, when our noble liberators desired me to go to you and urge you to uphold the Republican government, I told them this: that as long as you were still frightened you would promise anything, but as soon as your fears ceased you would be yourself again. When, therefore, the other former consuls were continually in and out of your house, I held to my opinion. And I did not see you on that day or the next. For I believed that good Romans could come to no understanding, could have no association, with a totally unprincipled enemy.

After two days had passed, I came to the Temple of Tellus – reluctantly enough even then, since armed men locked all its approaches. What a day that was for you, Antony! Even though you have abruptly turned against me, yet I am sorry for you – because you have subsequently done so little justice to your own good fame. If only you had been able to maintain the attitude you showed on that day, heaven knows, you would have been a hero! And the peace, which was pledged on that occasion by the cession of an aristocratic hostage – the young grandson of Marcus Fulvius Bambalio – would be ours.

Fear made you a good citizen. However, as an instructor of good behaviour, fear lacks permanency; and your unscrupulousness – which never leaves you unless you are afraid – soon perverted you into evil ways again. And indeed even at that time, when people (other than myself) had an excellent opinion of you, your manner of presiding over the tyrant's funeral – if funeral that ceremony can be called – was outrageous. For you were the man who pronounced that grandiose eulogy, that lachrymose appeal to morality. You lit the torches which charred the very body of Caesar, which burnt down the house of Lucius Bellienus. You, Antony, unleashed against our homes those ruffians, slaves most of them, whose ferocity we had to repel with our own hands.

And yet you seemed to have wiped off the soot. For upon the Capitol, in the days that followed, the resolutions that you proposed before the Senate were excellent. I mean those declaring that, from the fifteenth of March onwards, there should be no publication of any announcement conferring exemptions from taxes, or similar favours. As regards these exemptions, and the men in exile, you yourself remember what you said. But the finest thing of all was that you abolished from the constitution, for ever, the title of dictator. On account of men's recent fears of dictators you decided to abolish, once and for all, the whole institution: so tremendous was the hatred of this tyranny which had apparently taken hold of you.

So to other men the government seemed securely established – though to me things looked differently, for with you at the helm I expected all manner of shipwreck. Was I wrong? Could a man, for very long, remain unlike himself? Members of the Senate, what happened next you saw for yourselves. Announcements were posted up all over the Capitol: tax exemptions were put on sale, not merely to individuals but to whole peoples. Citizenship was granted not to single persons only but to entire provinces. If these decisions are going to stand, it means the downfall of our state. Senators, you have lost complete provinces. In his own domestic market, this man has slashed the revenues of Rome. He has slashed the Roman empire itself.

Those seven hundred million sesterces, recorded in the account-books of the Temple of Ops – where are they now? The origins of that treasure store were tragic enough. Nevertheless, if the money was not going to be returned to its rightful owners, it could be used to save us from property-tax. But how do you account for the fact, Antony, that whereas on the fifteenth of March you owed four million sesterces, you had ceased to owe this sum by the first of April?

Your people sold countless concessions: and you were well aware of them. Nevertheless, the decrees posted up on the Capitol did include one excellent measure. This concerned a very good friend of Rome, King Deiotarus. Yet all who saw the document could not help laughing, in spite of their grief. For no man has ever hated another so much as Caesar hated Deiotarus. He felt quite as much hatred for Deiotarus as he felt for this Senate, and the Roman knights, and the citizens of Massilia, and every other person in whom he discerned a love for the Roman nation and its people. In his lifetime Caesar never treated Deiotarus fairly or kindly, either to his face or in his absence. Yet we are invited to believe that, when Caesar was dead, Deiotarus gained his favours! When they were together, and Deiotarus was his host, Caesar had summoned him, demanded an account of his resources, planted a Greek agent in his principality, and deprived him of Armenia, which the Roman Senate had added to his kingdom. And now we are asked to believe that what the living Caesar had confiscated, the dead Caesar gave back.

And the way in which he is stated to have expressed himself! At one point, apparently, he described this restoration as 'fair'; at another as 'not unfair'. A peculiar way of putting the matter! I was not with Deiotarus, but I always supported him; whereas Caesar never once said that anything we asked for on his behalf seemed to him fair.

A bond for ten million sesterces was negotiated at Antony's house in the women's suite – where a lot of selling went on, and goes on still. The negotiators were the envoys of Deiotarus. They were good men, but timid and inexperienced. I and the king's other friends were not asked for our views. About this bond, I suggest that you should consider carefully what you are to do. For, when he heard of Caesar's death, the king himself – with no thought for any memorandum Caesar might have left – recovered what belonged to him of his own accord, by the strength of his own hand. Deiotarus was wise. He knew that this had always been the law: that when tyrants who had stolen things were killed, the men whose property they had stolen take them back. So no jurist, not even the man whose only client is yourself and who is now representing you, will say that there is a debt on that bond for what Deiotarus had recovered before the bond was executed. For he did not buy these possessions from you: before you could sell him his own property, he took it himself. He was a man! How contemptible, on the other hand, are we, who uphold the actions of someone whose memory we hate.

Of the countless memoranda, the innumerable alleged examples of Caesar's handwriting which have been brought forward, I shall say nothing. We can view their forgers, selling their efforts as openly as though these were programmes of gladiatorial shows. Today, as a result, the house where Antony lives is piled high with such enormous heaps of money that they have to be weighed out instead of counted. But this greed has its blind spots. For example one of the recently displayed notices exempts from taxation the wealthiest communities of Crete. This notice decrees that Crete shall cease to be a province 'when the governorship of Marcus

Junius Brutus comes to an end'. But where is your sanity, Antony? Are you fit to be at large? How could there possibly be a decree by Caesar exempting Crete 'when the tenure of Brutus comes to an end', seeing that in Caesar's lifetime Brutus had not yet even formed this connexion with Crete at all? However, do not suppose, Senators, that this consideration prevented the decree from being put on sale – indeed it has resulted in your losing your Cretan province! There was never a thing, provided a buyer was available, that Antony was not ready to sell.

And this law, Antony, which you posted up about recalling exiles – I suppose Caesar composed that too? Far be it from me to persecute anyone who is in trouble. My only complaints are these. First, that the men recalled from exile because Caesar had singled them out as especially deserving have been discredited by this new batch. Secondly, I cannot see why you do not treat everyone alike. Not more than three or four are now left unrecalled, and I do not understand why men whose plight is the same do not qualify for the same degree of your indulgence: I refer to your uncle and those whom you have treated like him. When you legislated about the others, you refused to include him. Yet at the same time you encouraged him to stand for election as censor! Indeed, you even encouraged his election campaign – thus arousing universal ridicule and protest. But, having done so, why did you refrain from holding his election? Was it because a tribune had announced an ill-omened flash of lightning? When you personally are involved, the auspices are immaterial. Your scruples are reserved for when your friends are concerned. And then, while your uncle was standing for membership of the Board of Seven, you deserted him again. Do not tell us that this was because of objections by some formidable member to whom you could not say no, for fear of your life! If you had any family loyalty, you ought to have respected Gaius Antonius like a father. Instead, you loaded him with insults.

What is more, you threw his daughter out of the house – Antonia your cousin. You had looked around and made an alternative arrangement. And not content with that, though no woman could have been more blameless, you even charged her with adultery! You could hardly have sunk further. Yet you were still not satisfied. On January the first, at a full meeting of the Senate at which your uncle was present, you had the audacity to declare that this was why you regarded Publius Cornelius Dolabella as an enemy: because you had learnt of his adultery with your wife and cousin. It would be difficult to say which was the most outrageous – your audacity in making such allegations before the Senate; your unscrupulousness in directing them against Dolabella; your indecency in speaking in such terms before her father; or your brutality in employing against that poor woman such filthy, god-forsaken language.

But let us return to the documents supposed to be in Caesar's handwriting. How did you verify them, Antony? To preserve the peace, the Senate had confirmed Caesar's acts – the acts which were truly his, not those which Antony alleged were his. Now, where do all these memoranda spring from? On whose authority are they produced? If they are forgeries, why are they approved? If genuine, why does money have to be paid for them? The decision had been taken that, from the first of June onwards, you should examine Caesar's acts, with the assistance of an advisory board. What was this board, and which of its members did you ever convene? And as for your awaiting the first of June, no doubt that was the day when you returned from your tour of the ex-soldiers' settlements: for you brought an armed guard to surround you.

That trip of yours in April and May, when you have even tried to found a settlement at Capua, what a splendid affair it was! We all know how you escaped from that town – or rather very nearly did not escape. And you are still uttering threats against Capua. I wish you would try to put them into practice: then that 'very nearly' could be struck out. Your progress was truly magnificent. Of your elaborate banquets and frantic drinking I say nothing; all that only damaged yourself. But we were damaged too. Even when, at an earlier date, the Campanian territory had been exempted from taxation, we regarded this as a grave blow to our national interests – although, on that occasion, soldiers were its recipients. But when *you* distributed land there, the beneficiaries were your fellow-diners and fellow-gamblers. Members of the Senate, these latest settlers in Campania were nothing but actors and actresses. Equally objectionable was the settlement at Leontini; seeing that at one time the crops in that area, like those of Campania, were renowned for their fertile and abundant contribution to the Roman domains of which they formed an integral part. You gave your doctor 1,875 acres. Whatever vast sum, one may ask, would you have given him if he had cured your mind? Your oratorical trainer received 1,250: what on earth would the total have been if he had succeeded in making a speaker of you?

But let us return to your journey, and to its effects on Italy. You founded a settlement of ex-soldiers at Casilinum, where Caesar had founded one before. About Capua, you had written asking for my advice; but I should have sent the same reply about Casilinum. You inquired whether it was legal to plant a new settlement where there was one already. I replied that the establishment of a new settlement, where there existed an earlier one duly founded in accordance with the auspices, was not legitimate – though I also pointed out that new settlers could be added to the old foundation. In spite of this, you had the arrogance to upset all the provisions of the auspices and plant a settlement at Casilinum, even though another settlement had been established there only a few years previously. You raised your standard; you marked out the boundaries with a plough. Indeed, your ploughshare nearly grazed the very gate of Capua, and the territory of that most flourishing settlement suffered grievous encroachment at your hands.

Fresh from this violation of religious observance, you rushed elsewhere: for you had designs on the property of the devout and high-principled Marcus Terentius Varro at Casinum. But what was the legal or moral sanction for this project? The same, you will say, as had enabled you to displace from their estates the heirs of Lucius Rubrius Casinas and Lucius Turselius – and countless others too. Now, if you had occupied these properties as a result of an auction, we may allow auctions their proper rights. We may concede rights also to written instructions, provided that they were Caesar's and not yours – and provided that they recorded you as a debtor, instead of releasing you from your debts!

As for Varro's farm at Casinum, who claims that this was ever sold at all? Did anyone ever see the auctioneer's spear or hear his voice? You sent someone to Alexandria, you say, to buy the place from Caesar. It was too much to expect that you should await his return! But no one ever heard that any part of Varro's property had been confiscated; and yet there was no man whose welfare was of more general concern. Now, if the truth is that Caesar wrote ordering you to hand the estate back, no words are fit to describe the outrage that you perpetrated. Just call off, for a spell, those armed men whom we see all round us. Do that, and you will very soon learn this lesson: whatever the justification for Caesar's auctions, your own deplorable conduct is on quite another level – for, once the armed men are gone, you will find yourself thrown outside Varro's gates. And it will not be the owner alone who expels you. Not one of his friends, his neighbours, his visitors, or his agents will fail to take a hand.

Day after day, at Varro's mansion, you continued your disgusting orgies. From seven in the morning onwards, there was incessant drinking, gambling, and vomiting. What a tragic fate for that house; and 'what an ill-matched master'!

Though how could Antony be described as its master?

Let us call him occupant. Well then, he was an occupant who matched it ill. For Marcus Varro had chosen this place not for indulgence, but for retirement and study. Those walls had witnessed noble discussions, noble thoughts, noble writings; laws for the Roman people, the history of our ancestors, the principles of all wisdom and all learning. When you, on the other hand, became the lodger – for householder I will not call you – the house rang with the din of drunkards, the pavements swam with wine, the walls dripped with it. On view were young free-born Roman youths consorting with paid boys; Roman matrons with prostitutes.

From Casinum, from Aquinum, from Interamna, came men to greet Antony. But no one was allowed in. And that was entirely proper, for in his degradation the emblems of office were a complete anomaly. When he left for Rome and approached Aquinum, quite a large crowd came to meet him, since the town has a considerable population. But he was carried through the streets in a covered litter, like a dead man. The people of Aquinum had no doubt been foolish to come; yet they did live beside the road on which he was passing by. What about the men of Anagnia? They, on the other hand, lived away from his path. But they too came down to greet him, on the supposition that he was consul. The incredible fact is – though I as a neighbour can vouch that everyone noticed it at the time – he did not return a single greeting. This was especially remarkable since he had with him two men of Anagnia, Mustela to look after his swords and Laco in charge of his drinking cups.

There is no need to recall to you the threats and insults with which he assailed the population of Teanum Sidicinum and harassed the inhabitants of Puteoli. This was because they had adopted Cassius and the Brutuses as their patrons. Their choice had been dictated by enthusiastic approval, sound judgement, friendly feelings, and personal affection – not by force and violence, which compelled others to choose you and Minucius Basilus, and others like you, whom no one could voluntarily choose as their patrons. Even as dependants you would be undesirable.

Meantime, while you were away, your colleague* had a great day when he overturned, in the Forum, the funeral monument which you had persistently treated with reverence. When you were told of this, you fainted: everyone who was with you agrees that this is so. What happened afterwards I do not know. I suppose terror and armed violence had the final word. For you pulled your colleague down from heaven; you made him quite unlike himself – to say you made him your own replica would be going too far.

And that return of yours to Rome! The whole city was in an uproar. Lucius Cornelius Cinna's excess of power, Sulla's domination we remembered; Caesar's autocratic monarchy was fresh in our memories. In those days there had been swords perhaps, but they had stayed in their sheaths, and there were not many of them. Your procession, on the other hand, was totally barbaric. Your followers were in battle order, with drawn swords,

---

. * Dolabella, now consul.

and whole litter-loads of shields. And yet, Senators, familiarity with such spectacles has inured us to the shock.

The decision had been taken that the Senate should meet on the first of June, and we did our best to attend. But we encountered intimidation and were abruptly forced to retire. Antony, however, feeling no need of a Senate, missed none of us; on the contrary, our departure pleased him. Without delay he embarked on his extraordinary exploits. He, who had defended Caesar's memoranda for his own personal profit, suppressed Caesar's laws – good laws, too – in order to upset the constitution. He lengthened the tenures of provincial governorships. Instead of protecting Caesar's acts, as he should have, he annulled them: those relating to national and private affairs alike. Now in the national sphere nothing has greater weight than a law; while in private affairs the most valid of all things is a will. Antony abolished both – laws, with or without notice; wills, although even the humblest citizens have always respected them. The statues, the pictures, which Caesar, along with his gardens, had bequeathed to the people of Rome as his heirs – now they all went to Pompey's gardens, or Scipio's mansion: removed by Antony.

And yet, Antony, you are so attentive to Caesar's memory; you love the dead man, do you not? Now, the greatest honours he ever received were the sacred couch, the image, the gable, the priest for his worship. Because of these honours, on the analogy of the priesthoods of Jupiter, Mars, and Quirinus, Antony is the priest of the divine Julius. Yet you delay, Antony, to assume these duties: you have not been inducted. Why? Choose a day, choose someone to induct you. We are colleagues; no one will refuse. Loathsome man! – equally loathsome as priest of a tyrant, or priest of a dead human being!

And now I have to ask you a question: *Do you not know what day this is?* Yesterday, in case it escaped your notice, was the fourth day of the Roman Games in the Circus. Now you yourself moved in the Assembly a proposal that a fifth day also should be added to these Games in Caesar's honour. Why, then, are we not in our official robes? Why do we allow the honour which your law conferred on Caesar to be neglected? You were prepared to concede, apparently, that this holy day should be polluted by the addition of a thanksgiving, but not by a sacred couch ceremony. But you should either disregard religious observances altogether, or maintain them invariably.

You ask whether I like this couch, gable, priest of the divinity. I like none of them. But you, who defend the acts of Caesar, cannot possibly justify the maintenance of some of them and the neglect of others. Unless, that is, you are prepared to admit that your own profit, rather than Caesar's honour, is your guide. Come, answer these arguments! I look forward to your eloquence. I knew your grandfather; he was a very fine orator. And you certainly speak with even greater freedom than he did. For he never made a public speech naked! – whereas you, straightforward fellow that you are, have let us all have a look at your torso. Are you going to let me have a reply? Are you even going to venture to open your mouth? Indeed, I wonder whether in the whole of my long speech you will find anything at all which you can pluck up the courage to answer.

But let us leave the past. Your behaviour today, at the present day and moment at which I am speaking – defend that if you can! Explain why the Senate is surrounded by a ring of men with arms; why my listeners include gangsters of yours, sword in hand; why the doors of the temple of Concord are closed; why you bring into the Forum the world's most savage people, Ituraeans, with their bows and arrows. I do these things in self-defence, says Antony. But surely a thousand deaths are better than the inability to live in one's own community without an armed guard. A guard is no protection, I can tell you! The protection you need is not weapons, but the affection and goodwill of your fellow-citizens. The people of Rome will seize your weapons and wrench them from you. I pray that we shall not perish before that is done! But however you behave towards ourselves, believe me, these are methods which cannot preserve you for long. Your wife – she is no miser, and this reference implies no disrespect – is already taking too long to pay the Roman people her third instalment.*

Our country does not lack men to place in charge of its affairs. Wherever they are, they are our national defence, indeed our very nation. Rome has avenged itself: but it has not yet recovered. However, that there are young noblemen ready to leap to its defence is beyond doubt. They may choose to retire for a spell, seeking quiet, but Rome will call them back.

---

* Her three instalments were her three husbands (p. 32, footnote).

The name of peace is beautiful – and peace itself is a blessing. Yet peace and slavery are very different things. Peace is freedom tranquilly enjoyed, slavery is the worst of all evils, to be repelled, if need be, at the cost of war and even of death. Even if those liberators of ours have withdrawn from our sight, they have left behind them the example of their deeds. They achieved what no one had ever achieved before. Lucius Junius Brutus made war against Tarquin, who was king at a time when kingship was lawful at Rome. Spurius Cassius Vecellinus, Spurius Maelius, and Marcus Manlius Capitolinus were killed because of the suspicion that they aimed at autocratic monarchy. But here, for the first time, are men raising their swords to kill one who was not merely aiming at monarchy, but actually reigning as monarch. Their action was superhumanly noble in itself, and it is set before us for our imitation: all the more conspicuously, because heaven itself is scarcely immense enough to hold the glory which this deed has made theirs. The consciousness of a noble achievement was reward enough; yet no one, I believe, should spurn that further reward which they have also won – immortality.

The day you ought to remember, Antony, is that day on which you abolished the dictatorship for ever. Let your memory dwell on the rejoicing of the Senate and people of Rome on that occasion. Contrast it with the haggling with which you and your friends busy yourselves now. Then you will realize that gain is a different thing from glory. Just as there are diseases, or dullnesses of the senses, which prevent certain people from being able to taste food: so, by the same token, debauchees, misers, and criminals are unattracted by glory.

However, if the hope of being praised cannot entice you to behave decently, is fear equally incapable of scaring you out of your repulsive behaviour? I know the lawcourts cause you no alarm. If that is due to innocence, you are to be commended. But if the reason is your reliance upon force, do you not understand this: that the man whose imperviousness to judicial processes is due to such a cause has pressing reason to feel terrors of quite another kind? For if you are not afraid of brave men and good Romans – seeing that armed satellites keep them away from your person – believe me, your own supporters will not stand you for very much longer. To be afraid of danger from one's own people night and day is no sort of a life; and you can hardly have men who owe you more, in terms of benefactions, than some of Caesar's killers owed to him.

However, you and he are not in any way comparable! His character was an amalgamation of genius, method, memory, culture, thoroughness, intellect, and industry. His achievements in war, though disastrous for our country, were none the less mighty. After working for many years to become king and autocrat, he surmounted tremendous efforts and perils and achieved his purpose. By entertainments, public works, food-distributions, and banquets, he seduced the ignorant populace; his friends he bound to his allegiance by rewarding them, his enemies by what looked like mercy. By a mixture of intimidation and indulgence, he inculcated in a free community the habit of servitude.

Your ambition to reign, Antony, certainly deserves to be compared with Caesar's. But in not a single other respect are you entitled to the same comparison. For the many evils which Caesar inflicted upon our country have at least yielded certain benefits. To take a single example, the people of Rome have now discovered what degrees of confidence they can repose in this or that person. They have discovered who are fit to be entrusted with their fortunes, and who, on the other hand, need to be shunned. Do these facts never occur to you? Do you never understand the significance of this: that brave men have now learnt to appreciate the noble achievement, the wonderful benefaction, the glorious renown, of killing a tyrant? When men could not endure Caesar, will they endure you? Mark my words, this time there will be crowds competing to do the deed. They will not wait for a suitable opportunity – they will be too impatient.

Antony: some time, at long last, think of your country. Think of the people from whom you come – not the people with whom you associate. Let your relationship with myself be as you please: but your country I pray you to make your friend once again. However, your behaviour is a matter for yourself to decide. As for mine, I will declare how I shall conduct myself. When I was a young man I defended our state: in my old age I shall not abandon it. Having scorned the swords of Catiline, I shall not be intimidated by yours. On the contrary, I would gladly offer my own body, if my death could redeem the freedom of our nation – if it could cause the long-suffering people of Rome to find final relief from its labours. For if, nearly twenty years ago, I declared in this very temple that death could not come prematurely to a man who had been consul, how much greater will be my reason to say this again now that I am old. After the honours that I have been awarded, Senators, after the deeds that I have done, death actually seems to me desirable. Two things only I pray for. One, that in dying I may leave the Roman people free – the immortal gods could grant me no greater gift. My other prayer is this: that no man's fortunes may fail to correspond with his services to our country!